"Interview With A Porn Star"

Jason Luke

Copyright © 2014 Jason Luke

Prologue.

The girl came from behind the tinted glass doors, out into the bright sunshine. She was naked. She had short blonde hair, a flawless tan, and breasts that were made impossibly perfect by surgery.

She came across to the recliner where I sat and stood over me, her slim teenager figure blocking out the mid-morning sun that was burning through the L.A. smog.

She cleared her throat to get my attention and there was a folded newspaper in one of her hands. She smiled sweetly. We had spent the night before together. Her name was Candy... or maybe Mandy.

She stood at attention for an instant and cleared her throat.

"Pisces," she said the word like it was an announcement, then began shuffling from foot to foot because the pavers around the swimming pool had baked hot. *"You've never been shy about speaking your mind, but for the next few days, it's going to come even more easily – and others will seem to be antagonistic. Since you love surprises, be ready for anything, from phone calls to unexpected visits to invitations to travel. You're always up for this sort of thing, but life won't be smooth."*

The girl lowered the paper and her face reappeared, still smiling.

"You've got good stars, Rick," she declared.

I ignored her. "What time is it?"

"After eleven," she said. "Why?"

I sat upright, swung my feet to the ground. "Because I have a reporter coming to interview me in less than an hour," I said.

The girl backed off a step, but her face became alight with mischief. She reached out and rubbed the front of my jeans boldly, her hand tracing the thick swell of my cock. I felt myself leap and pulse instinctively within the grip of her fingers. "Well, that still gives us plenty of time..."

I smiled a smile I didn't feel. I was hung-over. "Maybe some other time," I said blankly. "I'll call you, Candy."

The girl pouted with the spoiled expression of a child as I walked away. "My name's *Brandy!*" she called after me.

* * *

Chapter 1.

The knock was timid, almost reluctant. I fumbled with the buttons on the front of my shirt and cast a final quick glance around the living area, then opened the door, smiling.

"Hello," I said. "I'm Rick Cassidy."

The woman extended a hand. Her fingers were long and delicate, the nails polished and carefully manicured. I noticed a ring on one finger: a slim silver band with a tiny stone set into it.

The woman smiled nervously. She was older than me – maybe thirty-five. She had long dark hair, tied in neat braid so that the plait hung down between her shoulder blades. She was expensively dressed in a dark grey skirt and matching jacket over the top of a white blouse, distorted in its shape by the press of her breasts.

Her skin was pale, her figure slim. Her legs were long in sheer nylon, the heels making her appear a couple of inches taller.

She moved with a kind of anxious strain.

She smiled politely. Her eyes were sparkling green, with tiny flecks like gold around the edge of her iris. She was watching me intently with an expression I couldn't read. Maybe it was amusement, or maybe cool derision.

Or maybe it was a combination of both.

"Hello," she said, in a voice that was husky and cultivated. "My name is Connie Wright from '*Infinity*' magazine. I'm here for the interview."

I held the door open wide and ushered her into the cool of the house. She stood in the entry for a moment like a real estate agent inspecting a property. She turned to me and smiled. "It's a beautiful home you have," she said.

I smiled again but shook my head. The house was perched high in the hills overlooking the city below – but it wasn't mine.

"I'm only renting it for the next week," I explained. "The house belongs to a film producer friend of mine. I'm only making use of it until I finish my publicity commitments. Next week I fly back home."

The journalist looked politely surprised. "Oh? So where in the world do you call home?"

"Europe," I explained. "I have a property in France."

The woman drifted across the living room, her eyes taking in the expensive furnishings, the priceless artworks on the walls, and then a litter of empty bottles standing like soldiers on the kitchen counter. "France?"

I nodded. "I have a home there, and I've also built extensive film sets and production facilities," I explained. "And it suits my work. A lot of the actresses I use in my films are based in Europe, so it made sense to relocate there for filming."

The woman looked intrigued. "But you're an American, right?"

I smiled. "Born and bred," I confirmed. "I'm a Texan boy."

We stood there for a long moment in an awkward silence, as though – now that all the polite niceties had been completed – there was nothing left to say.

"Would you like to start the interview right away?" I asked, "Or would you like to see the rest of the house first?"

The woman had a handbag hung from a strap over her shoulder. She set it on a chair in the corner of the room and smiled again, her expression still filled with fluttering nerves. "I'd love to see the rest of the house," she said.

I led the way down the hallway, opening doors as I went and pulling back heavy drapes to show the breathtaking views of L.A.. The bedroom door was still open and the woman leaned across the threshold, saw the tangle of sheets strewn across the mattress and turned her head to me, one eyebrow raised pointedly. "I hope my arrival hasn't disturbed you?"

The question was a loaded one, with multiple layers of meaning that I chose to ignore.

"Not at all," I said. I pulled the bedroom door closed behind us and lead her out through the sliding glass doors to the pool area.

Set amongst landscaped gardens and concrete waterfalls was a good-sized swimming pool, the water crystal clear and sparkling blue. Nestled around the edges of the pool was a cluster of wrought iron chairs and a table, shaded by a bright yellow beach umbrella.

The woman made a clucking sound of approval in the back of her throat and turned to me. "This is spectacular," she said. "I had no idea actors in pornographic movies lived this kind of luxury lifestyle."

I frowned. "Really? What exactly were you expecting?"

The woman blinked and shook her head like the answer escaped her. "I don't know," she confessed. "I didn't really have any expectation – but I certainly didn't anticipate this!" She threw her hands wide in a gesture that seemed to encompass the house, the furnishings, the swimming pool and the surrounds all at once.

The midday sun was blazing hot. High in the sky overhead a jetliner began its descent towards L.A.X.. I took the woman gently by the elbow and escorted her back inside, into the cool of the house.

We stood in the living room for a moment, blinking our eyes until they adjusted to the cool gloom.

"Would you like a drink?" I asked.

The woman shook her head.

"Are you sure? I have everything – and I mean everything you could possibly imagine. Just name your poison."

She smiled politely, shook her head.

I went into the kitchen and cleared away enough empty bottles from the breakfast bar to set down a clean glass. I fetched a handful of eggs from the refrigerator, separated the whites and poured the slime into the glass. I stood by the kitchen counter for a moment, then chugged the concoction down my throat.

The woman looked at me like I was insane. "I can't believe you drank that."

I shrugged. "Egg whites are full of protein," I explained. "Most guys in the industry drink egg whites, or take a cocktail of herbs and vitamins."

"For stamina?" she sounded incredulous.

"No, for the money shot," I explained. "Lots of egg whites help in the production of semen. It creates a greater volume at the moment when I —"

She threw up her hands and clamped them over her ears. "I get it!" she said. "God, I get it."

I shrugged again, and then frowned, a little irritated. I stared at the journalist for a long moment and tried to remember her name.

"Connie..." I began carefully, "you know I am a porn film actor, right?"

The woman nodded. "Of course."

I shook my head. The frown stayed on my face.

The woman looked suddenly alarmed. "Why? Is there something wrong?"

I set the glass down aside. "Yeah," I said. "Your attitude."

The woman flinched like she had been slapped in the face. "My attitude? What do you mean?"

"You don't seem like the kind of lady who would be interested in interviewing a man like me."

"What makes you say that?" she became defensive. "Because I didn't want to hear about the size and strength of your come shots?"

I nodded. "There's that," I said, "and also your attitude when you saw the house. It was like you expected a porn actor to be holed up in some dingy, rat-infested apartment in the middle of a ghetto."

She stared at me, her gaze wavering and I could see some kind of turmoil going on behind her eyes. She propped one hand on her hip in a gesture of defiance and the tension stretched out. She took a deep breath. "Look," Connie said, "I don't have to like this assignment in order to write a good article. I'm a journalist, and I'm damn good at my job. I assure you, Mr. Cassidy, that my personal beliefs about what you do for a living will in no way affect my article."

"Your personal beliefs?" I antagonized her.

"That's right. My *personal* beliefs."

I came from behind the kitchen counter. "You don't like me, do you?" I asked casually. I lit a cigarette and tossed the lighter onto the counter. "You don't like me at all."

The woman hesitated, held my gaze for long seconds like maybe she was deciding how honest she could be. "No," she said finally. "That's not true. I don't know you – but I don't like what you are, or the industry you represent."

I exhaled a thin feather of blue smoke at the ceiling. "Is there a difference?"

"There is to me," she said. "I don't like the work you do, or the money you make from filming young women having sex. I think it's outrageous – abhorrent."

I nodded. "Fair enough," I said amiably. "But at least I'm honest, Connie. At least with me there is nothing fake, nothing untrue. Can you say the same about yourself?"

The woman didn't answer for a long moment. When she did, her tone was almost offended.

"Of course," she said.

"Really?" my smile became mocking but there was steel hidden behind the taunt. "You're a journalist," I said with scorn. "You people prey on the misery of others. Tragedy and horror are your stock-in-trade. Journalists sell millions of newspapers by spreading fear – and TV stations and magazines are just as bad. Journalists chase ambulances, interview the bereaved and invade the privacy of anyone... and they do it all in the pursuit of a story without any regard for the people who's lives they expose and profit from." The anger in me flashed like a spark, then burned out just as quickly. My tone became almost listless, my voice conversational once more. "So don't fucking lecture me about my career choice."

It was as if I had thrown a hand grenade. Suddenly, there was a black scorched crater of space between us. The woman stared and for long moments I expected her to snatch up her handbag and leave.

She didn't.

She didn't move.

I smiled. "Okay," I said brightly, shrugging off the last smoking tendrils of my anger. "Now that we understand each other, would you like to start the interview?"

The woman didn't move.

"Connie...?"

The woman blinked. Once.

I tried a different tack. I shook my head. "So, if you feel so strongly about the work I do, why did the magazine send you to do this interview?"

The woman finally stirred but I sensed her outrage was still smoldering. It seemed to take a great force of effort for her to smile, and when she did it was furtive. "It's a long story," she said with a sigh of breath she had been holding for minutes.

I nodded. "Tell me," I said.

She sat down on the sofa and crossed her legs. She took a long time to settle herself, re-gather her composure.

"When I heard about the chance to interview someone within the porn industry, I immediately volunteered," she explained. "That was a couple of weeks ago. But the editor gave the job to another journalist. That's who you were supposed to meet today – but she took ill at the last moment, and so the job was handed to me."

I thought for a moment, becoming offended. "So you didn't actually want to interview *me* – you just wanted to interview anyone within the industry."

She nodded, becoming awkward.

"Why?" I asked. "Why are you so interested in porn films?"

She didn't answer. Instead, she changed the subject.

"There must be a lot of men who would love a job like yours," she began, like she was buying a moment of time to organize her thoughts. "So what sets you apart? What makes you so successful and in such demand?"

I frowned, bemused. I stared hard at her. "You don't know?"

The journalist shook her head apologetically.

"I'm sorry," she confessed. "I wasn't expecting to interview you so soon. I normally research beforehand."

"At least you're honest," I grunted. I pushed myself away from the counter and stood before where she sat. "This," I said. I unsnapped the button of my jeans. I wore no underwear. My erection, half-hard, thrust out, swelling in size in an instant right before her shocked face. "Ten inches," I muttered. "Hard as an iron bar. That's what gets me the work — and that's why I'm known as 'Rick the Dick'."

Chapter 2.

"Are you okay, Connie? You look hot, and your face is flushed."

The journalist had her head turned away from me.

I tucked myself back into my jeans and refastened the zip and button, still smiling thinly. "Did I offend you? Is the sight of a man's hard cock something you find upsetting?"

The woman's lips were pursed, and she was staring away at the wall across the room. There were soft spots of color on her cheeks.

"Did I put you in an awkward situation?"

She turned back to me slowly and lifted her face to mine. "You could have put my eye out with that thing," she muttered dryly.

I nodded to myself. The woman was feisty. I liked that.

"You're going to be trailing behind me for what? Three days? Maybe four, right?"

The woman licked dry lips and then nodded. "Probably three," she said.

"Well then if you want to write a feature article for your magazine about who Rick Cassidy really is, you're going to have to accept me, and accept the way I live my life." I sat down on the sofa beside her and my tone became conciliatory. I patted her knee and she flinched, stiffened. Connie swiveled her head and looked straight into my face.

"How dare you," the journalist's voice suddenly became low and quivering. She glanced down at my hand on her leg, then back into my eyes. Her lips had turned frosty white as the blood drained away from her face. I felt a rush of reckless excitement at her reaction. Her anger was too swift and out of all proportion. I took my hand away from her knee, first letting my fingers linger on her thigh for long tantalizing seconds so that my touch became a caress.

Connie's lips remained a thin compressed line, as though there were angry words leaping to her throat that she was struggling to contain. I smiled and it was a taunt and a tease.

"My life is all about fucking," I said. "It's all about pleasures of the flesh, Connie. My life is one incredible sexual adventure with multiple partners and multiple positions. Every night – and most days – are filled with fresh young girls with tight hot pussies. It's what I live for. It's what makes me who I am. You need to understand that if you're going to write an article that is accurate... and honest."

Connie's eyes lit up with flickers of fire, and there was strange fury in the way she spoke to me, like a sparking fuse about to ignite.

"I do understand that, Mr. Cassidy," she hissed. "I'm a professional journalist. I've been writing feature articles about celebrities for many years... and I do accept that for the next few days there are going to be things I see and things I hear that may not meet with my personal approval, or align with my personal opinions," her voice rasped. "But let's get one thing clear right now," she held up an accusing finger and pointed it at the center of my chest. "I am not one of your fresh young

15

pieces of pussy. I am not the kind of desperate girl who would sell my body to you so that you could capture it on film," her voice began to rise and her tone became venomous. "So keep your hands off me, you arrogant bastard!"

I feigned a look of crest-fallen hurt. "Arrogant? Are you calling me arrogant?" My eyes became sad and injured.

"Yes," the woman flared.

I shook my head. "Well I'm not," I insisted. "I'm not arrogant at all."

And then I smiled. It was my best smile – the one I reserved for special occasions. It started at the corners of my mouth and spread across my face until it glinted mischievously in my eyes. "I'm cocky."

Connie almost smiled despite herself.

Almost…

I turned away, and as I did I glanced at the clock on the wall. It was well into the afternoon. Time for me to start drinking.

There was alcohol in the kitchen – a witch's pantry of potions that could be mixed to induce anything from euphoria to a coma. I decided on euphoria and started splashing spirits randomly into a glass and then stopped suddenly and tilted my head quizzically to the side. "Connie, I just don't get you," I said suddenly. "I don't understand where you're coming from. Are you deeply religious?"

The woman twisted on the sofa so that she could watch me. She shook her head. "No, I'm not religious at all."

I frowned as if the mystery had deepened. "Well, did you have a bad experience with a guy at some point in your life?"

The woman shook her head. "No."

I dropped a handful of ice cubes into the hideous mixture before me and then swallowed the contents of the glass in a single gulp. I winced as the fumes scorched the back of my throat, and I felt my eyes water. I hunched over the counter for a moment and waited until my senses stopped reeling and I felt the first soft glow of a buzz beginning to spread through my body.

"Well what the hell do you have against sex?"

Connie stared blankly for a few moments, like maybe she was trying to decide what she had against sex, or maybe like she was trying to decide if she should tell me. I watched her with bright eyes, my interest detached with a clinical kind of fascination. Curiosity made me want to know what made this woman tick.

"I just happen to think that sex is not something that needs to be — or should be — captured on film and shown to millions of leering men for their seedy pleasure," she said. "Sex to me can only come through a feeling of love, and a deep emotional need to share your body with another. But for you, Rick Cassidy, for you sex is nothing more than a cheap thrill. You treat the act like it's a disposable item. You don't value it," and then her voice trailed away so that I barely heard her whisper, "and you don't cherish it."

I felt a bemused laugh leap into my throat. I choked it down and shook my head sadly.

"It's sex!" I said. "Don't complicate it. Don't analyze it. And don't tarnish it."

"Tarnish it?"

"That's right," I pointed an accusing finger. "Sex is pure – it's an instinctive urge. It's as old as time itself – the coming together of a man and a woman to fulfill a basic and essential need. At least that's what it was before society burdened it with words like 'love' and the fucking church made the world feel guilty," I said.

The woman stared at me, her face blank, but something moved behind her eyes, like a cloud shadowing over a deep green lake.

"That's an interesting way of looking at things," she said cautiously, as if to concede the point somehow made her complicit.

"That's how I look at it," I said. "Sex is raw. Sex is real. Lust is an emotion we all feel. It shouldn't be demonized, it should be a celebrated part of life."

For a moment Connie's expression became ferocious and her dazzling green eyes snapped with a spark of electricity. She pushed herself off the sofa so that she was standing, facing me. "What about God?" she asked. "What about love and marriage?"

I shook my head. "I don't believe in any of them."

She paused for a moment, as though shocked or surprised. She arched an eyebrow and propped one hand on her hip. "Well what do you believe in then? What's left to believe in?"

"I told you," I said. "I believe in sex. It's the purest expression of who we are as people. Strip away religion and love, and what you have left is the only thing that matters – the only thing that truly inspires the best – and the worst in all of us."

Connie smiled but there was no humor in her face. The smile was bleak and merciless. "And what do you represent?" she asked me, becoming intrigued, almost challenging. "The best... or the worst?"

I hung a confident smile from the corner of my mouth. "Oh, I'm the best," I assured her, "In the most wicked, erotic way you could ever imagine."

Chapter 3.

Connie sat back down, the tension seeming to gradually seep away from her body. She settled herself on the sofa and when I looked next she had a notepad in her lap and a pen poised ready.

"So how do you want to do this?" I asked.

"This?"

I nodded. "How do you intend on conducting this interview? I mean do you have a list of prepared questions? Is that how you normally get your information and write your stories?"

Connie hesitated and then inclined her head just a fraction. "Normally..." her voice sounded almost self-conscious.

"Normally? Are you saying that I'm not a normal interview subject?"

She shook her head. There was the barest trace of a smile at the corner of her lips. "No," she said. "What I'm actually trying to say is that in normal circumstances, I would have a list of prepared questions to work from – but as I mentioned earlier, these circumstances aren't normal."

"Meaning you haven't had time to prepare and do your research, right?"

She nodded again as if to concede the point somehow diminished her. "That's right."

There was a big leather recliner chair in a corner of the room. I sat down so that we were facing each other, with just an oriental rug on the floor between us. I waved one hand in the air in a casual gesture. "No problem," I said. "Can't you just ask me questions today based on what you already know of me, and maybe some of my films you've seen? You can always do some research tonight and prepare questions, can't you?"

Connie shifted on the sofa with a kind of awkward agitation. I sensed her eyes become restless and remote.

"There's a problem with that," she said softly and I could tell by the tone of her voice that the words were an understatement.

I leaned forward. "A problem with what, exactly?"

Connie's face flushed and she swallowed hard. "I... I wasn't lying," she confessed. "I honestly didn't know who you were before yesterday when I was given this assignment... and I have never watched pornographic films."

I blinked in surprise, recoiled so that I slumped dramatically back into the chair.

"You've never watched a porn movie?"

The woman shook her head vehemently.

"Not even a glimpse – a scene or two?"

"No," she said. "Never."

I felt a sudden rush of indignation, my ire rising as I stared across the room and the woman held my gaze with a mixture of defiance and uncertainty. I stood up slowly.

"You arrive here with your puritanical standards about porn films and sex, and yet you've never sat down and tried to understand the thing you protest and complain about?"

Connie's eyes darkened. "I don't need to watch pornography to understand the evil that it causes," she said defensively. "I don't need to sit in some seedy back alley theatre filled with depraved old men to know that the industry preys on young girls and manipulates them for nothing more than cheap thrills and sick pleasure."

I sensed some mist of rage creep across my eyes – a concoction of alcohol and my own sense of disbelief.

"You know nothing about me, and you know nothing about the industry. Yet without any information to support you, you are prepared to tarnish the entire industry and paint it with the same broad brush stroke."

Connie stood up, shaking her head so that the braid swished across her shoulders like the tail of a big cat. "What about the complaints?" Her voice became adversarial, rising in a challenge. "There are endless complaints leveled at the porn industry, claiming that films such as yours only serve to objectify women – that women are being used in the most demeaning of ways merely for a man's pleasure?"

I waved my hand in the air, swatting away the question with weary content.

"Bullshit," I said simply. Years ago I would have been more defensive, more impassioned. But after a decade in the industry, I had heard this objection so many times I no longer bothered with a sterner response.

"The porn industry is diverse and massive," I said with my jaw clenched. "Aspects of the porn industry appeal to every fetish and fascination men *and women* have. Some elements of the porn industry focus on graphic acts beyond your imagination, and yet others emphasize the more subtle, gentler sides of sex and intimacy. You cannot put everyone in this industry in one group and label us all as seedy and depraved and demeaning towards women.

"In my films, I put women on a pedestal," I said. "I glorify women, not objectify them. I show them at their most passionate and most beautiful. They are the center focus of every scene."

"... Performing all matter of sex acts," Connie cut in.

I smiled thinly and shook my head. "No. Showing themselves as real women," I countered. "Showing them at their most vulnerable, their most powerful. Showing them as sexual and sensual – celebrating their femininity."

Connie huffed, seeming to bristle with antagonism. I saw words leap into her mouth, but I went on belligerently. "What sets my films apart, and what makes them the high-end is the budget," I explained. "I spend a lot of money, and it shows on the film. It's the opulent sets, the beautiful actresses I work with..."

"But it's still porn," the journalist cut across me defiantly.

"Yes," I said. "It's still porn – but the films are done tastefully," I defended myself. "We use two – sometimes three cameras – and everything is filmed in high definition."

"Yes," the woman countered. "But it's *still* pornography."

I wheeled around on her, suddenly irritated, and it took all of my restraint to keep my voice measured with reason.

"And the *'National Enquirer'* is a publication. So are all the glossy porn magazines. So is

'*Infinity*'. It's the quality of the journalism and photos that makes your magazine so successful. The same applies to my films."

She glared across the space at me. Electricity seemed to spark in the air between us. I could see her face filled with emotion and the hectic rise and fall of her breasts beneath the white blouse like she was trying to control her breathing and her temper.

"Okay..." she conceded warily. "But even if I accept that your productions are 'high end' porn, what about the other side of the coin? The seedy side of porn? There must be one."

"There is," I said grimly. "Back in the 80's, every porn film was shot on a set. There were cameramen, make-up people... even fluffers. Each film was staged, and there was more formal dialogue. But then the handheld camera came along, and so did free porn sites on the Internet. Suddenly, everyone was an instant porn filmmaker – and a lot of young girls got seduced and taken advantage of. It has become a generation of almost instant pornography. A guy with a handheld camera can throw a little cash at a desperate, young girl and film her. An hour later he can upload that footage. It's not tasteful, and the girls are forced to consider more desperate and outrageous acts if they want the work. If they hesitate, it's always easy to find someone else who is more desperate, or more gullible."

"What happens to those desperate gullible girls?"

I shrugged. "Invariably they get chewed up and spat out," I said. "They get used, abused and discarded."

Connie looked strangely bleak and disturbed. There was a frown of concern on her face.

"The girls get promised exposure," I said. "They are told that they are being offered a big break. They get told they are doing an audition tape and that – if they perform well enough – the footage will lead to work within the industry. Often it's a scam."

"I see..." Connie seemed to glance away and become distant, like her focus was elsewhere.

"After a couple of times, the girls either realize they are being used, or they become even more desperate. And naturally there are plenty of drugs and booze on the scene. A lot of these young desperate girls turn to drinking and drugs in order to perform the outrageous acts the guy behind the camera demands. If they stay sober – or lucid – they would never consider some of the things these guys expect of them. Drugs and booze numb the reality – for a while. Until it's over."

"That's why your industry has such a vulgar reputation," Connie said with her face screwed up into an expression of disgust. "Those sleazy opportunists preying on young girls – that's how everyday people view the world of pornography."

"I don't agree with you," I said flatly. "While I have to concede that there are too many scam-artists operating in the porn industry, they are the bottom-feeders – that scum at the very lowest levels of the porn industry. But, the porn industry isn't the only one to have its image blackened by opportunists with no morals."

"Is that so?" Connie's tone was acid.

"Look," I said with conviction. "The most common scam these predators run is the one I have already told you about — they set themselves up as fake agents, and they run ads in newspapers seeking young female models for adult work. When these impressionable young girls who are either desperate for cash, or have stars in their eyes meet with the guy, he tells them he has connections with the big studios, and the girl needs to shoot an audition tape," I said wearily. "Naturally, the girls think this is standard procedure. So the guy gets the girl to undress and puts a camera on her. Ten minutes later the guy makes it clear to the girl that he needs to know that she is capable of performing all manner of sex acts, because he wants to represent her and he needs to assure the studio that the girl knows how to suck and fuck."

I wandered around the room, frowning as I walked, gathering my thoughts. "Suddenly the girl is bent over the edge of this predator's desk with her panties around her ankles and him getting himself off by using her for sex. It's not nice," I made the classic understatement, "but it's what happens. After the girl has been used and humiliated, the guy wants nothing to do with her. He brushes her off with the old line about forwarding the tape to his contacts, and that he will be in touch with her. There might even be a promise of work... if the girl is naïve enough to subject herself to that kind of degradation for a longer audition tape."

I stood there for a moment in the middle of the room and then shrugged heavily. "That's the way it happens," I said and then my voice regained its bitter edge. "But this is not the only industry, Connie."

"You keep saying that," she challenged.

I gave her a wintry smile. "Maybe you should look at politics and the sleazy politicians who run this country," my voice had bite. "Let's start there, with all the double-dealing, and the corruption that takes place. Let's look at how many politicians have been caught up in sex scandals. Hell, even presidents aren't immune..." I let that remark hang in the air for a long moment. "And then you should turn your investigative journalist's eye towards law enforcement," my voice cut through the air. "How many cops have been dragged down and disgraced because they abused their power, or because they were corrupted by sex or drugs...?" I stood, like a defense lawyer pleading his case. "Do you really want me to go on?"

Connie was watching me, compelled by the passion in my voice, and her expression softened just a fraction. "But you're not one of those guys?"

"One of the sleazy ones?" I shook my head.

"You're not preying on gullible girls who are desperate for exposure and strung out on alcohol or drugs?"

I shook my head again. Connie sat down suddenly. "So what *are* you looking for when you're performing a scene with a woman?" She snatched up her notebook, flicked to a blank page and then peered up at me, pen in hand, with an air of expectation.

"Apart from a great pair of tits and a killer figure?" I taunted.

"Yes," she said dryly.

I smiled, then became serious. "I'm looking for passion," I said honestly. "I want a connection between me and the woman – a genuine attraction – and then I want that emotional chemistry to be captured on the screen for viewers to see."

"How?"

"Through the sex... through the woman's facial expressions. I want her to look hungry, aroused, even a little scared and unsure sometimes." I shook my head. "It doesn't matter what emotions they show, so long as they're real. So long as they're genuine. The porn industry of the past was full of bad acting and stilted female performers," I lamented. "The sex, the settings... everything about the porn of twenty years ago seemed fake and fabricated. It is the *one* benefit that has come about from the handheld camera. Because of it, we're able to shoot in exciting new locations without the need for truck-loads of production equipment, and we're able to move more freely around a scene, so that the viewer gets to see the action from angles that were impossible in times past."

The woman jotted notes as I talked, then looked up suddenly when I fell silent.

"But none of that matters if the actresses are still faking, right?"

"Right," I agreed. "That's the real key to my films. I take advantage of the new technology, and combine it with grand settings and actresses who aren't expected to act – they're expected to *interact*."

The journalist looked grudgingly impressed by my turn of phrase. She scribbled another note and then flipped the page of the pad resting in her lap.

"So how do you create interaction?"

I sighed. "It's not always easy," I admitted. "I try to work with girls I am comfortable with, and who are comfortable with me," I said. "Having an established relationship that we've built up over previous films makes the connection effortless each time we perform together. In other cases – if it is a new girl I have never met before – I try to spend some time with her when I am casting."

"You mean you have sex with her?"

I shook my head. "No. We just chat and I film her for a few minutes. I want to know in advance if the girl will be right for the scene I have in mind. I can sense that in their personality and in their attitude. The best women to work with are the nymphomaniacs and the ones who like to show off their bodies."

"Exhibitionists?"

"Yeah, they're the best women for porn films," I said. "The worst ones are the girls who are only working for the money, or maybe because they're curious. They generally only do a few films and then disappear. Porn is tough. You have to love your work, or you won't have any longevity in the industry."

Connie paused to write, and then looked up at me suddenly. She was frowning. "What about prostitutes?" she asked. "Have you ever worked with call girls? I imagine women in that line of work would be ideal for these kind of films."

I shook my head. "Hookers are even worse to work with than the ones who come on set just for the money."

"Really? I find that hard to understand."

"It's not," I explained. "It's actually makes perfect sense. You see prostitutes often feel ashamed of the work they do – and they definitely regard sex as just work. Sex isn't pleasure for them, it's their job, so they don't enjoy themselves."

Connie looked thoughtful for a moment. She flipped back through several pages of notes, rereading them silently while I watched. Then she looked up at me, her brow frowned in preparation for another question.

"What nationality of women do you think are best suited to the porn industry? Do you have any preferences?"

I nodded. "It has been my experience that women from Eastern Europe are more passionate and more in touch with their sexuality than women from the west," I said.

"You mean American girls?"

"I mean girls from the west in general," I said, side stepping any direct criticism of girls from the States.

"Why do you think women in Europe have that sexuality that you mentioned?"

"I don't think some women have a sexuality and others don't," I explained carefully. "I simply feel that women in Eastern Europe are more connected to that sexuality I believe all women possess within them. The girls in the west seem to have lost touch with that raw power." I shrugged. "Maybe it's because girls in the west have so many other distractions – the technology, the shopping – it's like they have lost touch with that part of themselves to a certain extent. The girls in Eastern Europe generally come from poorer economies. They don't have the same depth of distraction. Maybe that's why they have retained the sexual energy and instinctive feminine desire that manifests itself on film."

Connie made quick notes and then looked up again. "Have you made a lot of porn films, Mr. Cassidy?"

I smiled and held up a hand. "Call me Rick," I insisted.

Connie nodded cautiously. "Okay... Rick."

I kept smiling. "Yes," I confirmed. "Over three hundred."

She made a whistling sound of wonder through pursed lips. "That's a lot of sex."

"With a lot of women," I acknowledged. "And in many of my films I often have sex with several different girls in each scene."

She looked distracted and thoughtful, like maybe she was trying to work out the number of women I had been with. She was silent for a long moment, and then seemed to rouse herself.

"Do you have a favorite film?"

I thought about that. "No..." I said slowly. "I honestly can't pick out just one film. There have been so many I have liked, for different reasons. I love some films because of the locations we used. I love others because the women I cast were incredible. And there are others I like because my performance was best."

She frowned. "Your performance changes?"

"Yes."

"From film to film?"

"Yes, of course," I said. "It all depends on the women I am working with. Some ladies are not so much fun to do sex scenes with," I smiled wryly. "We just don't connect, and the scene falls flat because the energy is missing. Other girls are incredible. They make working with them easy."

Connie nodded, like she understood, but I knew she didn't.

She couldn't possibly understand.

Impulsively, I sprang from the big chair and crossed the room in three strides. I seized Connie by the wrist like we were running late for a date. "Come on," I said. "Enough talk. Enough theory."

I dragged her off the lounge and she trailed behind me reluctantly, a moment of alarm flashed across her eyes then faded just as quickly. "It's time you got to see for yourself what I have been talking about, and what you are determined to despise so much," I said. "It's time we watched some porn together."

Chapter 4.

The house had its own home theatre room at the end of the hall, and down a flight of steps. The room had been purpose-built in the basement, and the walls were sound-proofed. I leaned through the doorway and switched on the lights, then led Connie into a room that was about fifteen feet long and maybe a dozen feet wide. The walls were painted black, the ceilings dark wood paneling. There were three plush theatre seats in a line across the room, set before a massive television screen. I gestured for Connie to make herself comfortable, and I sat in the seat beside her.

"The monitor is connected to a state-of-the-art sound system," I explained. Built into the armrests of each seat was a console. I found the remote controls, and switched off the room lightning. For a moment we were plunged into deep silent darkness, and then the big television screen burst to life with music and a montage of erotic images.

"This is the film I wrapped up just last month," I explained. "We shot in Europe in a number of different locations, and did the post production work at my facilities on the farm. No one has seen the finished movie yet — it won't be released worldwide for another couple of months."

In the flickering light of the screen I could see Connie's expression, pensive and cautious. The music in the background swelled and then began to fade away and after thirty seconds, the title of the film appeared.

'A Hard Day's Night.'
Written and directed by Rick Cassidy.

"Wait!" Connie said suddenly. I felt her hand grope for my wrist in the darkness.

I stabbed 'pause' on the remote control and turned my face to hers. Light from the big screen played across the features of her face, softening them.

"*Written?*" she asked, bemused. "You take credit for writing a script?"

I looked at her, my features impassive. "Yes," I said. "Although it's not a Hollywood script," I conceded, "it's still a script."

Connie said nothing, and her silence was mocking.

I went on, "Writing, and planning a porn film is more about creating the atmosphere. It's more about trying to visualize and capture on paper the sense of the scene I want and the general dynamics, rather than specific dialogue," I said. "My films are all about reality – real emotions, and real settings, so it's impossible for me to write dialogue when so much depends on the interplay between the actors. Once I confine them to a script, I lose the spontaneity of what they really feel and say."

I pressed 'play' on the remote.

The screen faded to black for an instant and then filled again with a light, airy interior shot. The camera panned across an opulent room with marble floors. The furnishings were luxurious. There were elegant gold-framed paintings on the walls and clusters of delicate antique side tables. The camera slowly settled on an exquisite sofa, trimmed in gold and covered in plush velvet cushions. Perched on the edge of the sofa, sitting with her legs wide apart and her feet poised in impossibly high heels, was a beautiful young woman with long golden hair hanging down past her shoulders. She was gagged with a silk scarf, and there were leather bracelets about her wrists. She was wearing a high-collared top, the fabric so sheer that the shape and swell of her naked breasts underneath showed clearly through the gossamer silk.

The camera lingered on the woman's face and then drifted down to show the tiny patch of black lace between her parted thighs that covered her sex.

I leaned close in the darkened theatre room, my voice hushed. "We filmed this scene in a mansion on the Elbe River," I explained. "One of my production crew found the location and we filmed scenes non-stop for three days while the owners were in Paris."

Connie said nothing. Her eyes were fixed on the big screen, her expression astonished.

The camera moved almost reluctantly away from the pretty blonde, drifting left until a pair of black high-heels crept into frame. The camera followed the heels to reveal a second woman, laying on her back with her short skirt rucked up around her waist and her legs wide open. She was laying on the floor, her head propped on a cushion, dark hair fanned around her. The woman had her eyes closed, her lipsticked mouth open in a silent moan, and her fingers were thrust down inside her panties.

"That's Astrid," I said. "She's one of my favorite girls to work with. She's an absolute nymphomaniac."

In the background, the mic picked up the sound of footsteps, then panned back to reveal me, striding onto the set. I was wearing an expensive grey suit. I stood, my eyes admiring for a moment, and then the camera swung to the broad of my back and followed me as I went towards the girl on the sofa. She looked up into my eyes, her expression pleading. She held her hands out to me and I took them, lifting her to her feet. The girl on the screen leaned close and I wrapped my arms around her, letting my fingers slowly trace their way down over her bottom until I was rubbing the gap between her legs with my open palm. The camera swooped down, shooting the scene from between the girl's parted thighs as she began to rock her hips to press her sex harder against my touch.

"Emotion," I said suddenly to Connie. "These girls are eastern European. They don't speak English so everything has to be conveyed through their expressions. It's sexier than dialogue."

I saw Connie nod her head and then my eyes went back to the screen.

The blonde actress was moaning softly through the gag as my fingers pressed at the damp fabric of her panties that covered her pussy. The camera angle changed to show a wide shot and revealed the dark haired girl staring across the room at us in fascination. I turned the blonde girl's face towards the other woman, and whispered into her ear, "She's watching us. She's stroking her clit because watching us together turns her on so much."

The blonde girl's eyes became hooded and she leaned against me as though needing my support to stand. With my free hand, I untied the knotted scarf, and the gag fell away from her mouth. She gasped, and then closed her eyes and threw her head back. The camera angle changed again, coming in close between the girl's parted thighs to reveal my fingers now sliding deep within her, coated with the moistness of her arousal.

The shot stayed tight for long seconds, and then gradually panned back.

"I like to shoot sex scenes so that they flow," I leaned across in my seat and whispered to Connie. "One of the things I strive for is continuity. This scene you are watching now was filmed in one long take. I didn't cut and then recut – I simply filmed the sex as it evolved between myself and the girls on screen so that what you're seeing is what actually happened on the day of filming." I paused for a moment, glanced at the screen, then glanced back to Connie. "A lot of porn films are shot with just one camera, so they're constantly filming the same action again and again from different angles and moving the camera each time. I don't like to work that way because the sex loses its spontaneity. The only time the camera stopped during this scene was when we were building up to the come shot, because it's the most important moment of all, and it has to be filmed right."

On the screen, my hands were roaming across the blonde woman's breasts, pinching and teasing her nipples. The woman's mouth was open in a silent moan of pleasure, her eyes fixed on mine, intense and glazing with her arousal.

The camera came in for a close up of our faces as I kissed the blonde.

I leaned close to Connie once more. "Kissing," I said, as though the word was particularly significant. "It's one of the real secrets to my films."

I sensed Connie's puzzlement. "Really?" she asked, her voice hushed.

"Most porn movies get straight into the action – the physicality of sex," I said and then shook my head. "I don't. I take my time when I'm filming a scene to build up the sensuality and the eroticism. For me, kissing is incredibly arousing and full of passion. I want the viewers to understand that the motivation for the sex in every scene has its origins in passion – not just lust."

The camera angle changed as I broke the kiss and my mouth hunted down the girl's neck and throat. I tore her blouse open and sucked one of her hard pointed nipples between my lips. The actress arched her back as if to offer herself to me and I devoured her breasts as she entangled her fingers in the hair at the back of my head. The microphone picked up the girl's sigh of desire and then a smatter of language.

"She's Russian," I leaned across in my seat and said to Connie. "This film was the second time I've used her. She fucked one of my other actors in a film I made about six months ago. This was the first scene I'd worked with her personally."

Connie said nothing. Her eyes were fixed on the screen, watching the unfolding action as I wrenched the girl's panties down her thighs and then lead her to where Astrid, the dark haired woman, lay waiting.

The camera angle changed to show Astrid's view – looking up between the blonde's parted thighs as she stood astride her with me in the background, the tented shape of my hard cock thrusting stiffly within my pants – and then panned back to capture the three of us as the blonde slowly descended and her knees folded until she was sitting astride Astrid's face.

I knelt beside the women, my caressing fingers exploring along the length of Astrid's parted thighs while the blonde woman above her began to grind her hips slowly, rubbing her sex over Astrid's open mouth. The second camera showed a close up of Astrid's tongue flickering across the girl's swollen pussy lips as the blonde woman held herself open with her splayed fingers and undulated her body. When the shot finally cut to a wider view, I had peeled off my jacket and was standing naked but for my shirt. I was stroking myself gently, the length of me swollen hard and massive. The blonde turned her head, saw my erection and opened her mouth wide. I took a single step forward and began to gently thrust myself deeper and deeper into the Russian girl's willing mouth.

"See my arm?" I leaned across and nudged Connie's shoulder.

There was a moment's pause and then she whispered, "No."

"Exactly," I said. "As an actor in porn films, you get to understand very quickly about camera angles. What's happening on the screen is not for my pleasure – it's for the viewer's pleasure – and that only comes if they get to see the action. One of the first things an actor in the industry learns is to put his hand closest to the camera behind his back. That's not because it feels good," I grinned ruefully. "It's because it allows the camera an uninterrupted view of the action."

Connie said nothing, and I began to wonder if my commentary was wasted. There was a peculiar frown of concentration on her face, her expression almost entranced.

Almost...

I gave the cameraman long moments to get his shot and then eased my cock from the girl's mouth. It was glistening wet. The girl made a disappointed pouting face and then rolled her body away from Astrid until the two actresses were laying on the marble floor side by side, facing each other with their arms and legs entwined as though no one else in the world existed.

"Beautiful," I said impulsively. "Surely the most erotic thing in the world is two women in lust."

The angle stayed close on the girls kissing mouths, and then swept down their bodies as their hands and fingers began to explore. Astrid rolled the blonde Russian actress onto her back and the camera caught a wicked, sexy gleam in her eye as she moved her mouth down towards the girl's pussy. It was real. It was one of those treasured moments where the emotion could not be feigned. The hunger and desire in Astrid's eyes as she settled herself between the blonde's spread legs was right there on the screen for everyone to see.

The blonde girl reached down and pulled Astrid's mouth to her pussy, while I moved until I was kneeling between Astrid's spread thighs. I rubbed the swollen end of my cock against her flared welcoming lips and then slid myself deep within her pussy.

Astrid went stiff for an instant and lowered her head, as she became accustomed to the feel of my length sliding deep inside her. She turned her head, glanced over her shoulder at me, and her lipstick was smudged, her mouth wet with the blonde's juices.

I settled into a rhythm, the cameras moved for different angles, and for the next few minutes the action on the big screen was intense, building inevitably, so that when Astrid raised herself up on her braced arms I felt the sudden grip of her inner muscles as they began to contract around my cock. Astrid moaned — a raw husky sound torn from deep within her throat — and then she shook her head so that her long black hair broke in a shimmering cascade across her naked shoulders. The Russian girl came up onto her knees and crawled like a stalking cat around to my side. She opened her mouth and looked up at me with wide pleading eyes. I drew my cock from Astrid's pussy and slid it between the blonde's hungry lips.

The camera swept over the blonde girl as she took me deep into her mouth and then the lens captured a view of Astrid from between her spread thighs. Her long fingers were dipping in and out of her pussy. I waited for the shot to clear, and then eased myself back inside her.

With the blonde on her knees waiting patiently, I fucked Astrid with long thrusting strokes so that her whole body was rocked by the impact. She swayed like a tree before a rising wind and her moans and muttered whispers of encouragement became louder.

Again I sensed she was on the edge of her own release. I slid my cock back into the blonde's mouth to draw out the exquisite moment of Astrid's orgasm.

"That girl gave lousy head," I confessed in the dark to Connie. "She was all teeth and no technique."

I saw Connie turn her face. She stared directly at me. She sounded surprised. "You look like you are enjoying it."

I rolled my eyes. "Put that down to acting," I smiled. "In reality, all I was doing was playing for time. I like each scene to run for about thirty minutes, and I realized at this point of shooting that Astrid was close to coming."

"Is that so bad?"

"Yeah, it can be," I said. "Once the actress has orgasmed, the scene loses all its intensity and passion," I said. "The very best scenes are the ones where the girl reaches the edge but never quite releases. That way you are sure of passion and emotion right up until the money shot."

Connie almost looked distressed. "You like it when the girl doesn't come?"

"The film likes it," I said. "It's very hard to get lust and arousal on the screen when the woman you are fucking has had an orgasm ten minutes into shooting. Generally that burn of desire fades from their eyes and the chemistry between us is gone."

Connie shook her head. "That must be very frustrating."

"For me?"

Connie shook her head. "For the girls."

"It's the job," I shrugged, "and just because they don't come on film doesn't mean they don't come. After we finished shooting this scene, Astrid and this blonde spent an hour together getting each other off in the shower." I shrugged again. "The porn industry is like that. The sex that you see on the screen is not the only sex that happens. It's not like these girls just turn up, get undressed and spread their legs when the director calls 'action!' Often while we're waiting around to set up new scenes you'll find a couple of girls in the corner fingering each other or a girl going down on one of the guys..."

Connie looked like she was about to say something else but then the words just died on her lips as the screen filled with a close up shot of my cock forcing its way deeper and deeper down the blonde's throat. Connie's eyes were torn back to the screen as Astrid rose from her hands and knees and settled herself beside the blonde. The girls took turns sucking and stroking the end of my shaft so that the scene turned into an oral

43

competition between the actresses for the next few moments. Finally I fisted my fingers in Astrid's long black hair and held her head still while I began to buck and rock my hips. The blonde leaned forward and fluttered her tongue around the base of my shaft and the camera caught an exquisite shot of the two girls on either side of my cock, their lips kissing and touching deliciously as I felt my orgasm quickly building.

I pointed at the screen and clicked the 'pause' button. "This is where we cut," I explained. "This is the one moment where we paused filming to make sure I had cameras in the right places to capture the climax from every angle. You can't see it, but there are two other cameras set up – one over Astrid's shoulder, and I had a handheld camera filming the girls from above."

Connie turned her body in her seat so that she was facing me. "You filmed your own orgasm?"

"Sure," I said. "Point-of-view filming is something that has become common in porn since these little hand-held cameras hit the market – but that's mainly because you often have one guy filming, and it happens to be the guy involved in the scene. In fact, there is a whole genre of POV porn." I screwed up my face in an expression of disapproval. "It's not something I like," I admitted, "because I feel like it cheapens the quality of the film. An actor with a handheld camera can't keep the frame steady and concentrate on his orgasm at the same time – but because this is the money shot I need to make sure that it isn't missed, and that it is as compelling as possible for the viewer."

Connie gave me an artless, wry expression. "Compelling? Don't you mean graphic?"

"I mean compelling," I insisted. "Without the come shot at the end captured in an unique and interesting way, the proceeding twenty-nine minutes of film is wasted. It's nothing more than frustrating foreplay, or a book that has the final page missing."

I clicked 'play' on the remote, and a few seconds later the surround-sound speakers echoed my cry of release. There was an instant close up of my face. I was sweating, my jaw clenched, my eyes dark and intense, and then I threw my head back and growled at the ceiling. The scene cut back, and a moment later I exploded across the faces of Astrid and the Russian girl who were kneeling before me with their cheeks pressed close together, their eyes wide with excited anticipation, their mouths open and willing. I erupted, and the girls caught the essence of me in their mouths and on their chins. I reeled out of shot and the camera that had been poised and filming at my side swept in quickly to follow the girls as they embraced and kissed, their tongues lingering and lapping and swapping the taste of me until the screen gradually faded away to black.

We sat there in the darkness and the silence for long seconds. Without the light from the screen I could barely discern the shape of Connie's face, but I could sense that she was turned towards me and there was a peculiar gleam in her eyes.

It wasn't wonder.

It wasn't the look of some new-found sense of appreciation.

But maybe – just maybe – it was grudging respect.

"Well…" I asked. "What did you think?"

I heard Connie sigh, a soft exhalation of breath close by.

"Different," she conceded. "Very different to what I had expected."

"In a good way?"

"Yes," she said.

"How good?"

"In a good way that… that surprised me."

I was intrigued, and besides, a little praise once in a while does my ego no harm, so I fished for compliments. "What did you think of the sets?"

"They were much grander than I had thought."

"And the camera work?"

"Good," she admitted. "I didn't expect so many different angles."

"As I said, we use two cameras – sometimes three. I like to mix hand-held cameras with stationary cameras so that I get a variety of shots to choose from when it comes to editing."

She chuckled, but it was a giddy, slightly breathless sound. "Well you certainly didn't miss any of the action," she admitted. "Any closer, and…"

"Did you get turned on?" I asked.

Connie fell silent. The sounds of her breathing seemed to stop, as though trapped. "Was I supposed to?" she asked warily.

"Well, it is the purpose of porn."

Connie hesitated. "No comment."

I smiled to myself. "That's a dead giveaway."

"No, it's not," Connie leapt to her own defense primly. "It means nothing more than the fact that I am unprepared to answer you."

Chapter 5.

We emerged from the theatre room and I led the way upstairs, holding the door open for Connie with an elaborate bow of chivalry.

"What you just saw was one scene from my latest film," I said as she followed me down the hallway and back into the living room. It was late afternoon, and the sky had a smoldering, smoky haze to it. I stood at one of the big glass windows and stared down into the distant metropolis. "Each finished film has three or four scenes, so the running time is somewhere over ninety minutes. I like to give viewers value for their money. It was more important in the days of video where fans would purchase VHS from their local adult store. These days," I shrugged, "it's not so important. Most of my films are viewed or downloaded online through my website – but I still like the idea of value. I still like the idea that when someone watches a Rick Cassidy film, they feel it is money well spent."

Connie had a harried flustered look on her face. "Should I be writing this down?"

I shrugged. "I don't know. You're the journalist. What I'm telling you is not some kind of a prepared speech. I don't have a handout I can give you of all this stuff. I just say what I think and what I feel – when I think and feel it."

Connie waved a finger in the air like she'd had a sudden 'eureka' moment, or that I had said something profound. She stood, weight on one leg, hip cocked so that the fabric of her skirt was stretched tight across her bottom, and she scribbled quickly into her notebook. I waited until she looked up.

"Do you want that little speech about value again?"

She smiled and shook her head. "I think I have it," she said, and then she looked up at me suddenly as though struck by another spontaneous thought. "What's a fluffer?"

I did a double-take and frowned.

"You mentioned the word when we were talking about old porn films – but you never explained what one was or how it was used."

I started smiling but then stopped myself. "A fluffer wasn't any kind of equipment," I explained. "A fluffer was a girl who worked behind the scenes of a porn film, as part of the makeup department."

Connie frowned. "Like a hairdresser?"

I shook my head and lolled against the wall, my ankles crossed and one of my hands thrust into the pocket of my jeans. I smiled again, amused. "Not like a hairdresser," I said. "A fluffer was a girl who was employed to keep the male acting talent erect between shots when filming a porn movie."

"Erect… as in – "

"Exactly," I cut her off. "Sometimes on a porn set – especially when they were filming with one camera – it could be several minutes or maybe even half an hour between when they film one shot and when they moved the lighting and the camera to film the next shot. In that time the female actress might just lay on the bed waiting,

49

but the male actor had a problem. All the delays would mean he often lost his erection, so that when the director was ready to film again, he was faced with the prospect of talent unable to perform." I pushed myself away from the wall and crossed to the kitchen. All this talking was thirsty work. I needed another drink. I splashed bourbon into a glass, and didn't bother with ice. "To solve this problem a lot of production films included a fluffer," I said. "This girl got paid to use her mouth and body to keep the male talent aroused and erect so that when he walked back on set he was ready for action."

Connie stared aghast. "There were women who wanted to do that job?"

I nodded. "The money was good, and the girl's weren't ever filmed," I shrugged. "So I guess it had its benefits."

"Does it still happen? Have you ever used a fluffer on one of your films?"

"No. Never," I said. "Partially because of the way I film my scenes means there is no long delays between shots, and partially because I shoot with multiple cameras. And because of Viagra."

Connie said nothing. She was making notes as I spoke and she looked up at me as if to encourage me to continue.

"Viagra changed everything," I said. "Before it came along, male porn actors had a set of skills. Being able to perform in front of a film crew is not something every guy can do, and staying hard for an hour or two of filming is impossible for most guys. But since Viagra came along every guy thinks they can act in porn films. It's no longer a question of skill, or talent, it's simply a question of chemicals."

Connie scribbled furiously for several minutes and then glanced up at me cautiously. "Have you ever used Viagra?"

I shook my head. "No, I've never needed to, and when I do need a tablet to get a hard on, I'll walk away from this game for good."

I finished my drink, and splashed more bourbon into the glass. Connie set her notebook back down on the sofa and walked over to the big windows. I watched her, my eyes narrowed and appraising, admiring her lithe body and the way the clothes she wore accentuated her curves. She moved with feline grace and femininity. She stood at the window, staring out into the distance, as though her thoughts were miles away.

Her legs were long and slender, and the glaring afternoon light cast her figure in a silhouette.

"So tell me," I asked bluntly, "is there a man in your life, Connie? Someone who keeps your bed warm at night? I know you're not married – no wedding ring."

Connie turned from the window and gazed at me for a long silent moment and I saw wary caution creep into her eyes. She bit her lip like she was trying to decide how much she should tell me.

"There is," she said softly.

"Really?

She nodded.

"What's he like?"

Connie sighed, but the sound wasn't quite right. "His name is Robert," she said uneasily. "He works at the magazine."

"Oh," I was curious. "An office romance?"

She nodded but said nothing more, so I probed. "Is he a journalist too?"

"No," Connie shook her head. "He works in the advertising department as a high-profile corporate consultant."

I smiled, interpreting the official-speak. "So he's a salesman."

Connie said nothing. She folded her arms. The gesture lifted and pushed at the shape of her breasts, drawing them to my attention. Connie saw the direction of my eyes and her expression turned to ice. "He is a lovely, caring, considerate man," she said.

I nodded, still smiling. "I'm sure he is... but is he jealous?"

Connie laughed with a flash of contempt. "No," she said. "Robert has no need to feel jealous. He knows I adore him – and only him."

"Good!" I said. I slammed my empty glass down on the counter and wiped my mouth with the back of my hand. "Then he won't mind if I take you to dinner."

Connie froze. Her face filled with shock. "I beg your pardon."

I glanced at the wall clock, and tucked the tails of my shirt into my jeans. "I have a dinner meeting tonight with an old producer friend of mine – we're meeting at a little restaurant in L.A.. I thought you might like to come along."

"Have dinner with you?"

"Yes," I said, amused by the way her face was changing and contorting, dealing with the information and her perceived implications.

She balked. "I... I don't know..." she stole a peek at her wrist watch. "What time?"

I shrugged. "I'm meeting my friend at six... so any time after that. You can come with me right now, if you want."

"No!" she said, and then took a breath. "No – thank you."

I frowned. "'No' – you won't come to dinner... or 'no', you won't ride with me to the restaurant?"

Connie settled herself. I was toying with her, and she was beginning to become annoyed. "I'll come to dinner," she said stiffly, like she was accepting a formal invitation, "but I will meet you at the restaurant."

I nodded. I spotted a sports coat draped over the backrest of a kitchen chair. I shrugged it on, and made for the door. There was a chunky set of house keys on a side table. I tossed them to Connie as I left and she caught them in her hand.

"The restaurant is called *Mickey's*. It's off Sanders Street," I grinned. "Lock up when you leave. I'll get the keys back when I see you tonight."

Chapter 6.

'Mickey's' was one of those wonderful little restaurants that are dotted around L.A. — if you know how to find them. Well off the track beaten by the city's tourists, it was a quaint little eatery with a clientele of regulars who came for the food, but then came back because of the discreet surroundings.

There were no signs, and no menu in any window — just an on-street door that lead up a narrow set of stairs to a gloomy room with a low ceiling, dingy brown walls and thread-bare carpet. There were a dozen tables, and a counter across the far wall.

All the tables were full.

A young man with a brooding, sallow face greeted me at the top of the stairs. He looked Mediterranean. He had dark skin, dark hair. He was wearing an expensive suit. He looked me up and down carefully and gave the barest hint of a smile.

"Mr. Cassidy. Nice to see you again, sir."

We shook hands. "Good to see you, Nico. It's been a while."

The young man nodded, then glanced past me and indicated a corner table with a thrust of his chin. "Mr. Bellamy is waiting for you."

I smiled. "I have a lady-friend joining me a little later."

Nico nodded. "I'll send her to your table when she arrives."

I wove my way through the tightly clustered tables towards a dark corner of the room where a man was sitting alone. He saluted me with a raised glass and a good-natured smile. "Ah, the prodigal son returns."

He was a big man, broad and heavy across the shoulders, his voice like a low bass rumble of thunder. He was middle-aged. He had grey wavy hair and a fleshy face, the skin blemished with sun-spots and spidery veins. There were dark pouches of color below his eyes and the folds of loose flesh that hung from his jowls were stubbled with beard.

"Hi, John," I said. "I hope you're paying for this meal."

The man waved me to a chair with a hand the size of a baseball mitt. He was expensively dressed, but even the city's best tailors couldn't make a suit look good on his massive frame. He oozed that elusive unmistakable gloss of wealth — but he looked worn and rumpled, like something a dog had been chewing on.

"Sit down," John Bellamy said. "I ain't got time for your wise-ass comments."

I sat. A waiter glided across to my side and I ordered a drink.

Bellamy stared over the table at me, studying me with dark shrewd eyes. "You look good," he said at last.

I smiled. "You too," I lied. "It's been a long time."

The man nodded sagely. "Almost nine years."

I sat back in the chair and glanced around the room. The restaurant hadn't changed, and neither had many of the faces. I recognized some of the other diners – shadowy dark men hunched over their tables in earnest, secretive conversations.

I felt Bellamy's eyes on me.

"So, how you doin' kid?" he asked.

I shrugged. "I'm getting by," I said. "The film distribution deal is working out, and everything is fine back home."

Bellamy grunted. He was one of the porn industry heavy-weights – a man who could make or break a newcomer's career with a phone call. He was also my mentor. When I had decided to take the step from porn actor into the high-finance world of film producer, Bellamy had stood by me, discreetly in the shadows, and guided me through some stormy seas during those first few years.

I owed him.

I knew it.

So did Bellamy.

"You happy?"

I nodded. "Sure."

Bellamy looked hard at me, like he was trying to read my eyes, and asked his next question with elaborate caution. "You makin' a buck?"

I nodded. "A couple," I said.

Bellamy smiled – a knowing grin of understanding as he nodded his head heavily. "You're lucky," he said, and his expression became bleak and grey. "It's gettin' harder every day in this fuckin' business. Too many small fish," his voice became a bitter growl of protest. "They're screwin' up all kinds of things."

I frowned. "Small fish?"

Bellamy nodded. He was drinking neat whiskey. He drained his glass and then waved it in the air to attract a waiter's attention for a refill. "Fuckin' little production houses," Bellamy went on with a sigh. "They're cutting margins — producin' all this fuckin' reality shit."

I sat forward, lowered my voice. "You hurting, John?"

The big man looked up into my eyes. He nodded, and his voice dropped to a pained whisper. "Yeah," he admitted. "And I'm sick, Ricky."

"Sick? What kind of sick?"

Bellamy made a face, and scratched at the side of his hooked Roman nose. "The bad kind," he said, his voice a rusty croak. "The kind of sick I ain't gonna ever get better from."

I sat back in shock and for long moments we said nothing. The waiter came and poured more whiskey into Bellamy's glass. The conversations around us rose and fell in whispered undulations.

"Shit." I said at last.

Bellamy nodded. "Shit is right," he sighed, and then suddenly seemed to rouse himself, climb out of the dark hole of despair he was descending into. His eyes caught a spark of their old cunning glitter and a hint of a smile tugged at the corner of his mouth. "But it ain't all bad," he said. He sat up straight, arched his back and pushed back his shoulders, like a peacock preening itself. "I got myself a new girl."

"Really? I didn't know you had ended things with the old one."

"I haven't!" Bellamy suddenly laughed, and the spontaneous unaffected sound was like a loud bull-roar in the oppressive silence. It seemed to shake the walls, and heads turned, stared, then turned away again. Bellamy dabbed at his eyes with a paper napkin, then mopped away an unhealthy sheen of perspiration that had spread across his brow.

"She's nineteen," Bellamy shook his head in wonder. "She did a scene in one of my films. Man, what that girl can do with her mouth is fuckin' amazing!"

I smiled. "Congratulations," I said, because I didn't know what else to say. "Have you been seeing her long?"

Bellamy shrugged and then leered at me meaningfully. "Long enough to know every inch of her tight teeny body, but not long enough to remember her name."

It was the sort of thing I expected from John. The porn industry was a superficial world: the relationships were temporary, the sex faked. It was a world where pretty young girls were the kind of accessories that every successful business man had – more impressive than a flashy car or an expensive suit. A pretty young thing on the arm of an old man was a sign of prowess and power... and those two ingredients were the cogs that drove the industry.

The waiter came to the edge of the table and stood silent and discreet until Bellamy acknowledged him.

"Can I take your orders?"

"Fuck off," Bellamy said with a flash of charming smile. "We ain't ready."

The waiter turned a shade of grey and disappeared like a magician's assistant in a vanishing act.

Bellamy propped his elbows on the edge of the table and leaned close, his manner becoming suddenly grave and serious. He frowned and thrust his face close as though trying to study my expression in the gloomy light of the restaurant.

"I'm sellin', Ricky," he said at last. "I'm sellin' the whole organization – lock, stock and blonde, and I'm gettin' out."

I threw back my head with shock. "Out of the industry?"

Bellamy nodded. "And the fuckin' country. I'm movin' to Australia."

"Fuck…" I said in soft voice of disbelief.

Bellamy nodded again. "It's a young man's game now. All this fuckin' internet stuff," he shook his head, full of sorrow and worn down by his sickness. "It's time I got out and went somewhere sunny to die." He paused for a meaningful breath. "I'm sellin' to the Scarletti brothers… but I want you to do me a favor."

I fell back in the chair, stunned, reeling. I shook my head. "John, I can't believe you're getting out of the game."

"Believe it," he said. "The deal is done. There is just a loose end to tie up."

"Loose end?"

He nodded. "Like I said. I need a favor."

I had a sudden sense of wary suspicion. "I'll do what I can to help," I said, and then added with ill-concealed anxiety, "if I can afford it…"

He smiled, and then his expression faded to a rueful grin. "It's affordable."

"But — "

Bellamy held up his hand to stifle my protest. "Do I need to remind you that you owe me?" His mouth tightened.

"No, John. I know I owe you."

Bellamy pretended not to hear. He went on doggedly. "You fuckin' owe me for takin' you under my wing," he thrust a huge finger at me in accusation. "And you owe me for helpin' you get established, and gettin' a distribution deal, right?"

I nodded. "Right," I said.

"Then you help me out — with the blonde."

"The *blonde?*"

Bellamy nodded. "She wants to make it big in the industry. I told her you would use her in your next film."

I looked incredulous. "The new girl?"

He nodded. "She's one of them submissive types," he said in an off-hand manner, his voice dropping confidentially. "She'll suck and fuck whenever you want."

"John... I don't *need* another actress. And besides, you know I don't work with new girls. I only work with professionals."

He shrugged like he didn't care. "She's the favor. You fuck her, you film her, you put her on the cover of the DVD. It's what you owe me, boy."

I sighed. I glanced over my shoulder towards the exit, subconsciously looking for an escape.

Bellamy grunted, like he could read my mind. "How long are you in town for?"

I shrugged my shoulders. "A few more days."

"Are you filming while you're here?"

"Yeah," I said. "No point wasting the location. I've got some girls booked for tomorrow and Friday."

Bellamy looked pleased. "So that solves our problem," he said matter-of-factly. "I'll send this girl to you tomorrow. All you have to do is include her in one of your scenes."

I nodded. "Yeah, sure." I conceded unhappily. But Bellamy's hand shot out across the table, his grip surprisingly strong, the subtle warning in his tone unmistakable, though veiled. "Just make sure *you* fuck her, Ricky," he reminded me. "Not one of the hired cocks. I promised the girl that the one-and-only Rick Cassidy would do her. It's important if she's to get a name for herself. She's got to fuck some real talent if she's going to be taken seriously."

I was still shaking my head. I felt the floor beneath me beginning to sway and teeter.

I felt trapped.

I felt obliged.

I nodded my head. "Done," I said heavily.

Bellamy ordered another drink, and seemed to sink wearily back into his seat. At the same moment, Connie drifted into the restaurant. She wore a figure-hugging dress in bright oriental patterns that wrapped around her body tight as a second-skin. Her hair was brushed out, rippling and undulating like a black wave over her shoulders. She stood, uncertainly, for a moment, and then caught sight of me. Her face lit up with a flash of relief.

John Bellamy saw her at the same instant. He heaved himself upright in his chair, eyebrows arched with interest, and nodded meaningfully at me.

"Now that's something every man could enjoy fucking," he said, nodding his head, appreciation in his eyes. "She looks like the kind of ride that would give a man a great deal of pleasure."

I smiled wryly, but said nothing. I didn't need to. Connie crossed the restaurant and came over to our table. She grinned at me, then nodded politely to the big man sitting opposite. "Sorry, I'm late," her voice was breathless. "I had trouble locking your house up after you left me."

Admiring heads turned in my direction, and John Bellamy knocked over his drink.

Chapter 7.

It was eleven o'clock the next morning when Connie appeared at the front door, and by that time the house had filled with people. I had my makeup artist and two cameramen outside by the pool, and sprinkled throughout various parts of the house were four women and a couple of guys – all of them actors I had called in for a day of filming.

"Good morning," I held the door open wide.

Connie nodded. She was wearing blue jeans and a white open-neck shirt, the top button left undone so that as I glanced at her I could see the tight cleft of soft cleavage flesh that pressed against the fabric of her shirt.

"Did you enjoy dinner last night?"

Connie stepped into the foyer, glanced around the house, maybe sensing the buzz of activity. She nodded, her expression distracted with curiosity.

"Yes, thank you," she smiled. "Your Mr. Bellamy friend is certainly a character."

I smiled again. "John is a sleaze," I said matter-of-factly, "but he's also a straight-up guy, and he's well known within the industry. He has been a valuable ally for me since I came into the industry."

Connie tilted her head in a question. "Ally? Not friend?"

"Ally," I said. "I don't have friends – not in this industry anyhow. It's a tough business and I believe in the story of the barking dog."

Connie slipped the strap of the handbag off her shoulder and tossed it onto the sofa. "The story of the barking dog?"

I nodded. "It's a bit of an industry parable," I said.

"Tell me," she invited.

I closed the door and led Connie through the living room. It was a bright clear morning and warm sun through the big windows cut elongated wedges of sunlight across the carpet.

"There was this dog, and every morning when its owner fed it, the dog would bark its head off with excitement," I began. "Well it didn't take long for all the other dogs in the street to realize that whenever the dog barked it meant there was food in its bowl. So all the other dogs started jumping the fence each morning as soon as the dog began barking, and ultimately the dog starved to death because all the other dogs ate its food."

Connie stopped in the middle of the floor and stared at me. "That's the barking dog story?"

I nodded. "That's it."

She shook her head and then said slowly, "I don't get it."

I smiled. "The message behind the barking dog story is one for everyone who owns a business," I explained. "The point is that if you boast about how well you are doing everyone else is going to want what you have – just like the barking dog. So you keep your cards close to your chest, and you keep your mouth shut – and you don't make friends."

We stepped out through the sliding glass doors and I introduced Connie to my two cameramen and the lady who did makeup for the actresses. "They're all good people," I told Connie as we headed back inside. "Jilian, my makeup lady, has been with me for six years, and the two cameramen have been with me almost as long."

Connie had a bewildered look on her face. "Why are they here?"

"Didn't I tell you?"

"No."

I shrugged eloquently. "I'm filming today," I said. "I have six actors here getting ready in the bedrooms, and I'm planning to film a scene this morning and another one in the afternoon."

"Here?" Connie sounded shocked.

"Sure."

Connie shook her head. "But... but... you're going to film people having sex outside by the swimming pool?"

I shrugged my shoulders again. "Why not? It's a fantastic location, the weather is perfect for shooting, and we're high in the hills – it's not like I'm filming in a shopping mall."

"But... it's still out in the open."

"It's a great location," I said again. "And it's an opportunity to make a start on my new film before heading back to Europe at the end of the week."

A bedroom door opened at the end of the hallway and a young woman appeared. She had the bleary-eyed expression of someone who had slept fitfully. She glided barefoot into the living room. She was blonde, tall and tanned. Her hair was tousled, and she was naked. She scraped her fingers absently through her hair, and the movement of her arm changed the weight and shape of her breasts. She waved to me and smiled as she drifted passed.

"Good morning, Kate," I said. "Are the other girls awake yet? I want to start filming in an hour."

The pretty blonde shook her head, then disappeared through another door, closing it quietly behind her.

Connie raised an enquiring eyebrow. "How many other girls are in bed?" she asked acidly.

"Three more," I said.

Connie looked shocked. Her face became pinched and disapproving. "You shared a bed with four women last night? Had sex with them all?"

"No," I said. "Those four girls are actresses. They flew in last night and slept here – in their own beds and in their own room. They are here to perform in my film today."

"Oh," Connie said softly, admonished. Her eyes flicked away from my face guiltily. "I...I thought..."

"I know exactly what you thought," I said.

I left Connie standing there for a moment and went to the door Kate had appeared from. I knocked twice, and then stepped inside the room.

There were three young women in bed. Two dark haired girls were curled up together, and in a second bed a young red-headed woman lay on her back, naked, the bed sheets tangled around her feet. She had one arm thrown casually across her breasts, and her legs were splayed apart as she slept. I went to the bed and shook the girl's shoulder gently.

"Maxine," I said softly. "It's time to wake up. We are filming in an hour."

The girl's eyes fluttered open like beating butterflies wings, and there was a sleepy drowsy purr in the back of her throat as her vision swam into focus.

She smiled up into my face. "Good morning, Ricky."

"Morning," I said. "You need to get out of bed, honey. I need you on set as quick as possible," and then I added as an afterthought, "Wake up Kelly and Hannah."

When I came out from the bedroom, Connie was standing in the kitchen talking to two bare chested men. They had their hands thrust into the pockets of their jeans and were standing barefooted on the cold floor.

They were both good-looking men.

"I see you have met Roland and Victor," I said casually.

Connie looked up at me, slightly startled, slightly breathless, as if only just realizing I was now standing beside her.

"Not officially," she said.

I grinned and then went through the pantomime of formal introductions. "Roland and Victor – this is Connie. She is a journalist from '*Infinity*' magazine who is following me around for the next few days to write an article about me. Connie – this is Roland and Victor," the two young men held out their hands and flashed charming smiles. "They are porn actors. I've worked with them both before. They're good guys."

Connie blushed demurely and shook hands all around. There was a moment of awkward silence and then the two men drifted out through the sliding glass doors into the sunshine.

"Fascinating people," Connie said with the kind of stiff politeness that let me know she didn't mean it.

I smiled. "It's a fascinating industry, Connie." I meant it.

Connie followed the broad backs of the two actors with her eyes and then glanced back to me with a nod. "Are they good at their job?"

I inclined my head. "They can get hard on cue and hold an erection long enough to finish a scene," I said simply. "And they have good sized cocks. That's all I ask for."

Connie looked bemused. "Right. Right!" she said in a distracted way as if she had already forgotten the thread of the question. She fingered the top button of her blouse absent-mindedly.

Freud would have something to say about that.

"What about physical appearance?" she asked. She leaned her hip against the kitchen counter. Her expression became a frown of concentration. "I mean porn films are filled with gorgeous buxom lithe young girls... doesn't the physical appearance of a male porn actor matter just as much?"

I shook my head. "Not at all," I said. "It's all about the cock," I explained. "The physical appearance – the facial features – of a man makes no difference in a porn film." I shrugged offhandedly. "It's a bonus if you can find a guy with a decent physique, but that's not even really important."

Connie folded her arms and narrowed her eyes in a challenge. "That sounds like blatant hypocrisy," she huffed. The color of her eyes had turned glacial.

I felt a bristle of temper. "It's not," I said. "It's about understanding and identifying your audience – and the majority of my audience are men. Those viewers don't care what the guy looks like. He could be a grotesque, two-headed monster – it wouldn't matter at all. All the guys are looking at when they watch a porn film is the girl." We were standing toe-to-toe, me towering over her, but Connie's body was rigid with tension and defiance. "When I film, I focus on the girls," I went on. "The guy might get one close up, and that's usually his facial expression when we shoot the money-shot. Apart from that, every minute of screen time is dedicated to the actresses, their expressions, and the sex. If the guy appears on camera, it's because he's part of the scene. But he's never the focus of the scene."

"Well that's sexism, then," Connie growled persistently.

"Bullshit," I said. "It's sex... without the 'ism'."

There was a defiant snap behind Connie's eyes and I could see angry words leap to her lips. I saw her expression flicker and change, and then gradually lose its ferocity.

She let out a long breath, like a boiling kettle lets off steam, restraining herself with a visible effort. She smiled at me but the expression was thin on her lips.

"Do you feel that porn films serve to objectify women?"

I frowned. "Jesus!" I said. "You sound like one of those conservative fucking feminists who scream at the top of their lungs every time women portray themselves in some way that is remotely sexy."

Connie's expression darkened. "I am not advocating that opinion, Mr. Cassidy. I'm merely asking the question of you. I want to know your opinion on the matter."

"My opinion? I'll tell you my opinion," I said grimly. "I don't know whether porn should bare the brunt of feminist criticism for objectifying all women as merely sexual playthings," I said. "I think *if* women have been objectified then men are not entirely to blame. For a woman to be portrayed in a sexual way, the woman herself needs to be willing and compliant. You might want to blame men and blame porn for the way some people perceive women, but I don't think it's that simple."

Connie gazed at me evenly. "What about you personally then?"

"Are you asking me whether I objectify women in my films?" I asked, my voice becoming lower and more resentful.

"No," Connie said carefully. "I'm asking you whether you see women as sexual objects. I think it's a fair question considering the work you do."

I nodded, and my demeanor changed in an instant. "I think that's a fair question too," I admitted, and then said truthfully, "yes."

Connie looked shocked. For long seconds her expression was blank, and then it began to fuse into a scowl. "You do? You admit it?"

"Yes," I said, and then went on quickly. "When I first meet a woman, my initial opinion of her is formed in a sexual way," I said. "I assess her on the basis of how she would look naked and performing in one of my films."

Connie's scowl became a look of outrage. "That's not an opinion many people would admit to."

I shrugged. "It's the truth," I said. "But," I stabbed a finger into the air, "I believe I have that opinion because of the work I do."

Connie looked disbelieving. She gave me a venomous glare. "Making porn films gives you the right to undress every women with your eyes the moment you meet them?"

"Yes," I said.

"How can you justify that?"

"My objectifying of women is not because I am a man, or because I am sexist," I explained patiently. "I objectify women because of my profession, in exactly the same way that a real estate agent walks into a house and their first thoughts are for the features of the home and what price it might fetch on the market." I went on, hammering home my point. "My objectifying of women is exactly the same as a chef going to a restaurant for dinner. His first thoughts are for the quality of the food and the way it is presented.

In every case our profession dictates the way we think. My profession is all about women and sex. How else would you expect me to think?"

Connie flapped her hands like sails that had lost their wind. She became suddenly fascinated with her fingernails, until the angry color had drained from her cheeks.

"When I got home last night, I went over my notes from yesterday and it occurred to me that I'm going to need some publicity shots to go with the article," she said to change the subject and steer it away from the dangerous waters we had been floundering in. "Do you have any photos I could use?"

I nodded. "If you want a set of stills from any of my films, I can have them sent to you," I said as I crossed the living room and reached into a desk drawer. "But I have these publicity photos if they will help."

I laid several large color photos of myself out on the desk like playing cards. In one of the images I was standing naked, facing the camera with my arms folded. My penis hung long and heavy as a lead bar between my braced legs. I had shaved my crotch before the shoot – a trick to make everything appear even larger. In the image I was tanned dark brown. The photo had been taken in France twelve months ago. Since then the tan had faded, but the bulges and ripples remained.

"Oh, shit!" Connie gasped. She reeled away, her eyes enormous, her mouth agape. She clutched at her throat with one hand, a warm red flush spreading across her face.

"Don't you have any publicity shots of yourself *clothed*?" she asked. Her voice was reedy and breathless.

"Why?"

Connie stared at me, stunned. "Because these are so... so confronting!" she explained. "They're almost vulgar."

"Vulgar?" I wasn't sure I'd heard her correctly.

She nodded her head vehemently.

My lips pressed into a thin bloodless line and anger blazed behind my eyes, so that when I spoke my words were a simmering hiss. "If I was a cop, you would want photos of me in uniform. Same if I was a solider or a pilot. If I were a scientist, you would expect to photograph me at a desk behind a telescope – and if I were an astronaut, you would want to photograph me in my spacesuit. This," I stabbed an angry finger at the photos, "is me in my uniform. This is my work – my career. I'm not ashamed of what I do, Connie," I felt my temper simmering, right at the brink of boiling over.

Connie seemed to recoil, maybe shocked. There was a peculiar blankness in her eyes, edged with the residue of her defiance.

"They're tasteless," she said softly.

I blinked.

I stared.

Then I snapped.

"You know something," I said suddenly, "you're a very rude woman."

Connie glared at me. She flinched, and a flush of color spread hot across her cheeks.

"How dare you criticize me," my voice crackled like a bushfire. "I didn't ask for this interview – your magazine requested it. The last thing I expected was to be judged by some arrogant, narrow-minded woman who has a grudge against the porn industry."

Connie stood, rooted to the spot. The color in her cheeks blazed and the expression in her eyes became disconcerted.

I lost the last of my control.

"Fuck off," I said with an impulsive hiss of decision, and the final shreds of Connie's bravado collapsed in an instant. I snatched up her handbag and hurled it through the open front door. It hit the top step and landed in the garden. "I don't need to be interviewed by '*Infinity*' magazine." She seemed to cringe beneath the lash of my voice. I seized Connie by her wrist and marched her out the door.

Slammed it closed behind her.

That felt good.

I closed my eyes, threw my head back and let out a long tense breath – shrugged off the anger like a heavy cloak.

I heard the patter of light footsteps behind me and opened my eyes to see a naked young woman coming down the hallway with a radiant smile on her face. She had long dark hair, and exotic features. Her voice was a sultry purr.

"Ricky, darlink!" the woman threw her arms around my neck and pressed her breasts against my chest. Her accent was European, her English fractured. She kissed me hot on the lips, and then leaned back and smiled into my eyes. "I've missed you very great much," she said. "Will you be fucking into me today?"

"Hannah, you look beautiful, baby," I said with a smile that never reached my eyes. My arms were resting lightly on the woman's naked hips. She molded her body against mine shamelessly.

"You fuck me, Ricky?"

I shook my head and pretended to be saddened. "Not today, I'm afraid," I said. "But Roland and Victor will give you all the cock you need."

Hannah screwed up her face into a petulant, sulky pout and I felt her hand high on my thigh and then her fingers grope for me. "This is all the cock I need," she whispered. Her eyes were enormous and inviting. She licked her lips with the tip of her tongue and then began to rub my length with the palm of her hand.

I took a step back, held her at arm's length with my hands on her shoulders. I gazed into her eyes. "Hannah, nothing would make me happier than another chance to fuck you, baby," I put a hint of hardness into my voice. "But I've already worked out the scenes we are filming today, so we're just going to have to wait for another time."

Hannah made a disgruntled huff in the back of her throat. She shrugged theatrically. "Okay," she said. "But can I have Maxine then?"

I nodded and smiled. "Deal," I said. "You can play with Maxine before the two guys take turns with you."

Hannah flashed me a deliciously wicked little smile. "This is good," she said huskily and nodded her head.

There was a sudden rap at the front door, and I narrowed my eyes. I left Hannah standing naked and flung the front door open, expecting to see Connie standing in the doorway.

She was. But she wasn't alone.

Standing beside Connie was a blonde teenager, with a Californian tan and a mop of long curly blonde hair. The girl flashed me a brilliant white smile. Her eyes were big and blue, her lips painted red. The girl was wearing a yellow sleeveless top that was cut off about three inches above her navel, and a pair of skin-tight denim shorts. The young girl's face lit up with recognition.

"You're Rick Cassidy."

I nodded. "I know," I said. "Who are you?"

The girl cupped her hands beneath her breasts and then ran her splayed fingers all the way down her body to her hips like she was smoothing out the wrinkles of a dress. "I'm Lily," she smiled. "John Bellamy sent me. He promised you would fuck me."

I raised an eyebrow in recognition and then nodded. I held the door open and the girl drifted passed me in a cloud of cheap perfume. I stood there. Didn't move. Connie stared at me.

She was standing on the bottom step, a tragic kind of haunted expression in her eyes.

"Rick... I'm sorry," she said, "I went too far. I was rude."

My expression stayed stony. "Fuck being rude," I said. "You were *unprofessional.*"

Connie nodded, and lowered her eyes, chastened. When she looked back up at me, she had her bottom lip trapped between her teeth. "Can we start again – from the beginning?"

I held the door open for her and she came up the stairs, relief obvious on her face. She stood in the middle of the living room floor like an uncertain visitor. I waved her over to the sofa. "Take a seat," I said.

Connie perched herself on the edge of the sofa, feet flat on the ground, knees pressed together, sitting upright and attentive. She had her hands clasped in her lap, kneading her fingers with anxiety.

"Listen, Connie," I began reasonably. "I get it. I understand. You don't like me, and you don't like the work I do." I waved a hand in the air. "But if you're going to hang around with me for the next few days, there are some things *you* need to understand." I crossed the living room floor and perched myself on the edge of the desk. "First, I expect you to do your job – nothing more, nothing less. That means I don't want to hear you criticize my lifestyle. It also means I don't want a commentary," I stared her hard in they eyes. "Just observe... and then vilify me and demonize me in your article – but until then, you hold your fucking tongue unless it is to ask questions. Clear?"

Her face flushed hot and red. "As a bell," she said tightly.

"Good." I slid off the desk and snatched up a half-glass of whiskey that someone had left on a table. I swallowed the contents in a single gulp and then winced. The stuff tasted like drain cleaner.

"Now, I have to film two porn scenes today," I kept my voice level and controlled. "The first one I am shooting this morning," my eyes flicked to the wall clock and I realized there wasn't much of the morning left. "That scene is going to involve two of the girls and the two men that you met in the kitchen. This afternoon," I began to pace back and forth across the room, "I am going to do another scene with two other girls and that pretty blonde who was on the doorstep when you were leaving. I have to fuck the blonde."

Connie tilted her head. "*Have* to?" she asked delicately.

I nodded. "Have to," I confirmed, "as a favor to John Bellamy," I said. I glanced over my shoulder, suddenly wondering where the blonde had disappeared to. She wasn't anywhere to be seen. "I promised John I would fuck her because she wants to make it in the industry, and to do that she needs to be screwed by some big names. That's how a young starlet gets a reputation these days."

Connie's expression became inquisitive. "Yesterday you told me that you didn't like working with inexperienced actresses."

"I don't," I said grimly. "I don't like working with any girl I don't know, and I'm not comfortable with. I don't have the time to waste filming some empty-headed bimbo who knows nothing about camera angles, and nothing about performing on film."

"But you're going to do it anyhow, right?"

I nodded. "I don't have a choice," I said. "This industry is like a house of cards — it's held together by a network of favors and paybacks. If someone does you a favor, you gotta pay back the debt. I owe Bellamy for the help he gave me way back when I started producing my own films. Fucking this young girl for him is payback."

I went hunting through the house for the girl and found her in the bedroom, laying on her back with Hannah lying beside her. The two girls were kissing passionately, and Hannah's experienced fingers were between the young blonde's spread legs, cunningly teasing the folds of the teenager's shaved pussy. The young girl had her eyes closed, her lips parted in a soft silent moan, while in the bed beside them another of the actresses was sitting quietly with her back against the wall. Her legs were spread and her knees were bent, her fingers dancing lightly across her sex while watching on.

I stood in the doorway for a long moment.

Despite myself, I felt my erection growing thick within the confines of my jeans. Girl on girl sex is my weakness, and I gazed upon the intensely erotic scene until Hannah tore her lips from the blonde's and began to trail wet kisses over the teenager's breasts towards her parted thighs.

Okay... Maybe just a few more minutes...

Hannah swept back her long hair from her face and held it behind her neck as she began to gently lap her tongue along the glistening folds of the young blonde's pussy. The girl arched her back and gasped a breathless moan. Her tiny hands fisted into the bed sheets and then her breath seemed to lock tight in the back of her throat as

Hannah moved her mouth to the sensitive nub of the girl's clit.

"Sorry to interrupt your fun, girls," I said at last, with genuine reluctance. "But I need everyone outside and ready for makeup. You can continue this after filming."

When I came back into the living room, Connie had made herself more comfortable on the sofa, seeming more relaxed now. She had her notebook open in her lap. "Did you find the blonde girl?"

I nodded. "She was in one of the bedrooms having sex with one of the other actresses."

Connie blinked, flinched. "*Actresses?*"

I nodded casually. "Sure," I said. "Just about every porn actress is bisexual. In fact, it's just about a job requirement. Most guys are like me, Connie. The one male fantasy that seems a common thread between all guys, is the idea of seeing two beautiful young women enjoying each other's bodies on a bed," I said. "That kind of bisexual interaction is something that's very, very common on film." I dropped onto the sofa beside where Connie sat and turned my face to hers. "In fact, I don't think a girl could work in this industry unless she was into other girls as much as she needs to be into fucking guys."

Connie did a thing with her mouth, but said nothing. Instead, she glanced down at her notes and then back to me.

"Do you have time to answer some questions?"

I glanced at the clock on the wall again. "A couple," I said. "The rest will have to wait until after I shoot this first scene."

From the corner of my eye I caught a flicker of movement and Connie and I both turned our heads as all five girls came down the hallway. They were all naked, and unaffected by their nudity. Hannah and the blonde had their arms comfortably around each other's waists. The girls paraded passed us, wiggling hips and flirtatiously jiggling their breasts as they filed out through the glass doors towards the swimming pool area.

Connie had a distracted, peculiar expression on her face. She blinked as though to clear her mind.

"You said all the girls in the industry need to be bisexual if they want to work, right?"

I nodded.

"What about gay men in the industry?"

I shrugged. "What about them?"

"Well, how do you feel about it?"

"It makes no difference."

"None at all?"

I sighed. "Look, I happen to think the sexiest thing in the world is the sight of two beautiful women in each other's arms, kissing and exploring each other's bodies with their fingers and tongues. Lesbian scenes are the greatest turn on... and I'm not the only guy who feels that way."

Connie nodded. "I get that," she said, "but what about gay men?"

I shrugged my shoulders again. "The gay scene is a large part of the porn industry," I said, "and good luck to them. I have no problem with gay men working in porn."

Connie sounded persistent. "But do you like gay men?"

"I do... I just don't want them to hold it against me!" I quipped.

Numb silence.

"It's a joke," I said.

More numb silence.

I sighed. "Maybe not a funny one..."

Connie fixed me with blank eyes. "I'm laughing on the inside," she said dryly. "And I'm trying to be professional."

Touché.

Connie's hand raced across the page as she made notes. When she looked up again, ready to ask her next question, I cut her off abruptly.

"Have you ever been married, Connie?"

She arched her eyebrows, like maybe the question was too personal for her to want to answer. She gazed at me steadily for a long, appraising moment, then nodded.

"Once," she said softly.

I frowned, intrigued. "Once... as in you have been married one time, or once... as in 'once upon a time'?"

"Once upon a time," she said stiffly.

I nodded. "A long time ago?"

She smiled bleakly, like even now the memories were still painful. "A very long time ago," she sighed. "I was only eighteen. The marriage didn't even last two years."

"You divorced him?"

She nodded. "We separated for a while, then tried again after a few months passed but nothing had changed. He was still the same guy. I never saw him again."

I got up and went to the big desk. In the top drawer were a dozen cigars. I clipped the end off one with a pocketknife and moistened it between my clamped lips. "Have you always been a journalist?"

Connie nodded. "For the last fourteen years," she said. She shifted her weight on the sofa, and crossed her legs. They were long legs, perfectly shaped.

I lit the cigar and drew on it until the tip was burning evenly. A trail of blue smoke drifted in lazy tendrils towards the ceiling.

"Have you always worked at '*Infinity*'?"

Connie shook her head. She had set her notepad aside and now her hands were clasped in her lap. "When I first started out, I was working as a reporter on local newspapers. I didn't start working on magazines until a few years ago."

"You prefer magazines to newspapers?"

"I do," she said. "The magazine format gives me a lot more freedom as a writer. I found the newspapers too restricting and impersonal. There was only ever enough space to write the facts. With a magazine, I have a lot more page to fill, but a lot more room to explore the subject."

There was a loosening within the shape of her body, as though she had begun to relax now we were talking about a subject she was comfortable with. Her face became more animated and her personality began to shine through that confronting façade.

"The writing style in a magazine is a little more creative and casual," Connie said. "I like that. I enjoy being able to express myself with less limitation. I feel it makes for a more interesting article."

I glanced at the big clock and realized that filming couldn't wait any longer.

"Connie, I want to talk to you more — but I have to shoot a scene, and if I don't start filming now I'll never get to the second scene later this afternoon." I got up from the sofa, and then as an afterthought I turned back to Connie and reached out my hand. "Do you want to come and watch this?"

Connie's eyes went from my face, to my hand then back to my face. There was a tiny frown of hesitation on her brow, and then it faded away like a passing cloud and her face lit up into a bright smile. It wasn't the kind of smile to make a man's heart melt — it was the kind of smile that guests wear when they go to a party they don't really want to attend. "Sure," she said.

Connie took my hand like that pretty wallflower who gets asked to dance at a high school prom, and I led her out onto the pool deck.

Chapter 8.

If it wasn't midday yet, it was awfully close. The sun was high overhead, the view down into Los Angeles smudged in haze, like a scene filmed through a soft focus lens. I waved everyone over to me.

"First scene," I held up my hand for silence, "will be Maxine and Hannah with Victor and Roland."

The two actors nodded, and Hannah gave Maxine a provocative little smile. "The rest of you girls will perform with me in the second scene I shoot later this afternoon. For now you three ladies can go inside and enjoy yourselves. There's plenty of booze and plenty of bedrooms. Do whatever you want to entertain yourselves, but get the fuck off this pool deck," I delivered that last line with a smile to take the edge off. "The last thing I want is one of your pretty asses popping up in the background, okay?"

I turned to Jilian. She was a woman in her mid-thirties, with high Slavic cheekbones, and platinum long hair. She had made a couple of porn films about a decade ago, and she still retained her stunning looks and amazing figure, but in the last ten years she had also developed enough common sense to realize that getting laid on film wasn't ever going to be a long term career. Now she was a makeup artist – and a damn good one.

"Jilian, I need you to finish up with these girls as soon as possible," I said.

She nodded. "Five minutes, Rick," she said.

"Good. Not a minute more."

I turned to Hannah and Maxine, and then did a quick double take back to Jilian. "Is the makeup waterproof?"

Jilian frowned, shook her head. "Sorry, no."

I waved it off. "No bother," I said, formulating the scene I would film in my mind. "We'll take a different direction."

I turned back to Maxine and Hannah. "You two girls will be laying on recliner chairs by the side of the pool," I said, "when Roland and Victor appear from inside the house. They are going to come over and chat to you both for a couple of minutes before the sex starts. Clear?"

Both the girls nodded. Jilian started fluttering around them with brushes and paint, but I hadn't finished issuing instructions. "I want this scene to have a lot of girl-on-girl action," I said. "Maybe you girls can start kissing as the scene opens and then Maxine, I want you to start fingering Hannah's pussy when the boys are over talking to you. The rest of the action can unfold from there, but I need you two guys..." I stabbed a finger at Roland and Victor, "...to get these girls into lots of lesbian situations. Get 'em on their hands and knees kissing. Get one of the girls squatting over the other's mouth... you know the kind of thing I'm looking for, right?"

Victor and Roland were standing at the edge of the group with their arms folded, their upper chests oiled by sweat and sunlight so they looked like bouncers at a club for male strippers. They were professionals, and I knew I could trust them

86

both to perform to my instructions once I called 'action!'

The girls drifted away to the lounge chairs, and Jilian floated around them, putting the final touches to lips and eyes. Victor and Roland disappeared inside to await their cue, and I turned my attention to my cameramen.

"Guys, let's try to get this in one take," I said. "Walter, fetch me one of the handheld cameras. I will be shooting this with you."

I took Connie by the elbow. "Stay right behind me," I said. "I'm going to be filming this scene with the boys, and I want you to get a sense of this aspect of the industry. Maybe, seeing it the way a cameraman sees the scene will give you a new perspective... and maybe even an appreciation."

Connie said nothing. She didn't even make the effort to smile this time.

I took the handheld camera and everyone got into position. Jilian disappeared through the sliding glass doors with a makeup case in her hand and another one tucked awkwardly under her arm. Less than a minute later, Victor and Roland came sauntering out onto the deck and filming started.

Maxine and Hannah were stretched out casually on two recliner chairs close to the edge of the pool. Hannah propped a pair of dark glasses atop her head and leaned over her chair to kiss Maxine. I let the camera linger on the girls, panning slowly along their bodies while still holding Roland and Victor in the background. Hannah deftly slid a bikini strap off Maxine's shoulder and her hand cupped the red head's breast. Maxine's nipple was hard.

The two men got to the side of the chairs and crouched down, their gazes admiring and hungry. Maxine's bikini disappeared and the girls finally broke the kiss, feigning sudden surprise to see the two guys at their side. Maxine gave Victor a sexy wink and Hannah playfully pushed at his chest.

"No, she is all mine," Hannah said. "You cannot have her."

She sucked Maxine's nipple between her lips, her eyes open, still watching the men. I moved my camera to get a shot of Maxine's face, her eyes closed, her mouth open, and a soft little moan of arousal escaped her lips, right on cue.

I moved position, sensing Connie shadowing my steps. Maxine's thighs had fallen open. She was wearing a tiny bright yellow bikini and I could see the cleft of her sex through the tightly rucked fabric. Hannah's hand drifted down the flat of Maxine's abdomen and her fingertips disappeared inside the waistband of Maxine's bikini bottoms.

Roland stood up. He was rubbing his cock through his jeans. He took a step towards where Maxine lay on her back and unzipped his jeans. His cock sprang free from the confines of his pants, swollen and hard. He stroked himself gently and then shifted his weight and moved his hips so that his cock slid across Maxine's parted lips. Instinctively her mouth opened wide, and her eyes became narrow, knowing slits. The pink tip of her tongue flicked along the ridged length of

Roland's shaft and his body clenched and pulsed to this new sensation.

Maxine's hand drifted up along Roland's thigh and then she took him gently in her grip and her fingers began to flutter along his cock in time with the soft teasing of her lips. Her legs fell wide open and Hannah's hand reached down inside her bikini bottoms and began to massage her sex.

Victor was an experienced porn actor. He knew enough to be patient: he knew enough not to crowd the scene, and so he stayed on his haunches, playing the part of an admiring voyeur until Hannah had stripped off Maxine's bikinis and she lay sucking Roland's cock with her legs spread wide apart.

"Go down on her, Hannah," I said. "Get between her legs and lick her."

Hannah moved with the fluid smoothness of her experience. She didn't glance at me — she simply eased herself off the recliner chair and crawled on her hands and knees to where Maxine lay. Hannah was wearing a black bikini, and Victor waited until Hannah's face was buried between Maxine's legs before he got to his feet and stripped off his pants.

When Victor reached down and rubbed Hannah's pussy, the girl lifted her lips from Maxine's sex and turned her head. She winked and smiled an invitation, and then shuffled her knees apart so that Victor's hand was free to remove her bikini.

"Take your time, Victor," I grunted. "Fuck her slow, because I want plenty of close ups."

Victor settled himself on his knees by the edge of the pool. His cock was in his hand. He stroked it a few times until it was rigid and swollen, and then guided the head of himself up and down the moistening slit of Hannah's pussy.

I moved in close and got down on one knee so that I could film the moment Victor first eased himself inside Hannah, and then panned back quickly to capture the expression on the dark haired girl's face. Hannah played it up perfectly – screwing her eyes tightly shut, her mouth falling slack and open, and the husky moan in the back of her throat one that suggested that the feel of Victor's cock inside her was the most magnificent sensation she had ever experienced. Her chin was slick and glistening with the juices of Maxine's pussy.

I moved position again, going for a wide shot, while my other two cameramen circled the four actors like vultures – swooping in for close ups and then circling high and wide. Victor was driving his cock deep inside Hannah with deliberate slow strokes, and when the dark haired girl suddenly reached back between her legs to cup his swaying sack in her hands, Roland seized his opportunity to draw Maxine down onto her hands and knees.

Maxine's pussy was already wet. Roland seized her by the hips and plunged himself inside her.

"Take it easy," I growled a warning at Roland. "She can't kiss Hannah if you are pounding into her like a fucking jackhammer."

Maxine grunted. She lifted her face and the two girls came together in a grinding kiss that bumped and broke as if they were kissing in the back seat of a car on a potholed road.

"Better," I said.

The guys had settled into a workable rhythm – thrusting their hips with enough impact to sway and rock each woman's bodies, but not so fiercely that the girls were unable to lock their lips together. All three cameras caught the action from different angles until, after several minutes, Victor eased his glistening cock from within Hannah and she turned around with an eager hungry mouth.

Hannah's cock-sucking technique was epileptic: furious, wild action without a great deal of direction. She was crazy. I kept my camera in a close up as her mouth ravaged Victor's cock, and when I sensed the guy was close to coming I called a sudden halt and shut the cameras down.

"Come shot," I said and then waved my arm around as I gave instructions. "Maxine come and kneel beside Hannah, please. I want Victor to shoot his load over both your faces and then we'll end with a come swap, okay?"

Both girls got into position kneeling before Victor's braced legs. Their mouths were open wide like hungry chicks waiting to be fed. Victor stroked his cock slowly, and then fed the length of his shaft to Maxine. Maxine's mouth wrapped tight around Victor's length and she swallowed him whole, until the tip of her nose was nuzzled against the washboard flat of his abdomen. I got a great shot of Victor throwing back his head with his eyes screwed tightly shut and then Maxine's mouth slipped off the end of his cock just as he bucked his hips and released.

The money shot was a good one. Victor's come splashed over the girl's faces and they turned, wrapped in one another's arms, and kissed in lewd unaffected delight, their tongues twisting and slithering between their open mouths.

"Nice!" I said as Victor reeled away and I was able to press in close with the camera for a final shot of the girls. Come had dripped from their chins and was spattered across their breasts. Hannah scooped the last of Victor's seed from Maxine's breast with her fingertip and sucked it into her mouth.

I called 'cut!' and there was a round of applause for the actors.

Roland put one of his hands up. He was stroking his cock with the other hand. "Where do you want it, boss?"

I thought about that for a moment. Filming a come swap was the most common way to end the scene – because it was the most popular with viewers. But not every scene can end the same way...

"We might do this one as a cream pie, Rolly," I decided. "Maxine, honey, get yourself comfortable on that recliner chair again."

It took several minutes before we were ready to shoot again. Maxine stretched herself out like a sacrifice on an alter, and spread her legs wide. Roland knelt between her thighs, and when his cock was deep inside her the cameras starting rolling again. Hannah was kneeling close beside him with one arm wrapped around his waist and her free hand strumming Maxine's clit. Without the need for restraint, Roland clenched his jaw and growled. He had his hands on Maxine's hips, fingers digging into the firm flesh. Maxine thrashed her head from side to side and pinched her nipples until finally Roland's whole body went into a rigid seizure.

The camera caught the tension in Roland's face: the muscles in his chest flexing, the corded ropes standing proud in his neck — and then the sudden rush of release that melted away the hard strained edges of his features as he relaxed suddenly.

Roland staggered out of the shot, and I pushed in close for a tight shot of Maxine's shaved pussy. The lips of her sex were swollen and flared wide like the petals of a flower. As I pulled the camera back I caught Hannah licking her lips the instant before her tongue flicked out to lick at Maxine's pussy. There was a look of delight in her eyes.

I held the camera close, caught the sights and sounds of Hannah lapping at Maxine's sex for several moments and then gradually pulled back for one last wide shot.

"Cut!" I cried — and a moment later regretted the decision.

Hannah kept licking Maxine's pussy.

This wasn't for the movie — this was just red-hot girl on girl sex for no other reason than because they were into each other.

I waved urgently to Walter, and we both started filming.

The girls seemed completely oblivious to the cameras. Hannah's tongue was deep inside

Maxine's pussy and the red head had her back arched, sucking in short panting breaths. One of her hands glided down her body and her fingers entangled themselves in Hannah's hair to press the girl hard against her undulating pelvis. Hannah grunted. Her eyes were closed. She was still on her hands and knees. Somehow she managed to reach down between her own legs to finger-fuck herself.

"I come soon!" Maxine's voice was ragged. Russian, Belgian, or even Chinese – even if you didn't speak the language, you could tell by the delicious torture in Maxine's expression that she was on the verge of orgasm.

Hannah made a humming sound that came from somewhere deep in her chest. Her eyes opened and we all saw the instant of Maxine's release as the rapture of her orgasm contorted her features into something breathtakingly beautiful.

I kept filming.

I shot long minutes of the two actresses kissing tenderly as Maxine drifted down from the clouds of her ecstasy.

I kept filming.

I videoed the girls embracing, their hands wandering over each other's soft curves until Hannah rolled onto the hard sun baked pavers and Maxine crawled between her legs.

I kept filming.

I zoomed in tight as Maxine lowered her mouth to Hannah's thigh and her lips fluttered soft kisses all the way to the core of her lover.

Hannah turned her head to the side, eyes closed, and there was a dream-like smile on her lips until Maxine's mouth found her clit and Hannah flinched and then bucked with urgent arousal.

"Oh, God. Yes!" the words burbled up from Hannah's throat. Walter brought his camera close to Hannah's face and kept it there while I moved to film the touch of Maxine's tongue on her pussy.

It was great footage — that priceless, genuine moment that was rare in reality, and even rarer on film. Hannah's body began to ripple, and then the crashing waves of her orgasm dashed against her and left her spent and exhausted.

Maxine turned her face slowly to the camera. She licked her lips with a blissful expression of guilty pleasure.

"Cut," I murmured softly.

I shut the camera down and handed it to Walter. I turned, and Connie was standing there, right behind me. There was a hectic flush of color on her cheeks and something decadent in her eyes. She glanced passed my shoulder to where the two actresses lay, and then her eyes shifted back to mine.

"Well? What did you think of that?"

Connie shook her head, made a wide-eyed expression. "I honestly don't know what I think," she said.

I frowned. "How do you feel?"

She made a mouth like she was gulping for air. She sounded breathless.

"I... I thought it would be like some kind of perverse lecherous scene... like the kind of thing men in dark raincoats would watch through bedroom windows," Connie said. "I thought it would be like a vulgar voyeuristic thing..." she tried again.

I watched her, bemused.

She shook her head. "But it wasn't like that at all. I found myself being quite disconnected from the sex," she confessed. "Even though I didn't have a camera in my hand, watching what just took place became like a practical exercise – moving around to film from different angles felt more like a function rather than a creepy fantasy."

I shrugged. "I'll take that," I said. "At least you didn't hate it."

"I don't think the finished scene you put in your movie is anything I would ever watch, Mr. Cassidy... I'm not saying that," Connie insisted primly. "What I am saying is I can understand that in your role as a filmmaker, I now appreciate that making movies like this is not some sleazy way to get cheap thrills – it seems to involve a lot more creative and practical considerations than I had first expected."

I threw my head back and laughed, and then impulsively slapped her on the shoulder. "Spoken like a fucking politician!" I smiled. "You just said a whole lot, without saying a damn thing at all."

Connie pursed her lips. Apparently she had decided she had said more than enough.

Chapter 9.

The shade of the living room was a cool relief after filming in the midday sun. I went straight to the kitchen and filled a glass with whiskey. As a compromise to the heat, I dropped in two cubes of ice.

"Would you like something to drink, Connie?"

She nodded. "Anything non-alcoholic, thanks."

I screwed up my face. "Shit... I don't know if we have anything that doesn't contain alcohol."

Connie smiled thinly. "Water would be fine."

I carried her drink to her, and we stood close together in an awkward uncomfortable silence like strangers on a blind date. Muted sounds of water running hummed in the background. Connie cocked an ear.

"Shower," I said. "Everyone will be taking turns, or maybe even sharing the shower."

Connie nodded and did a thing with her lips that made it clear to me that she didn't want to know anymore. So I explained...

"After we film a scene everyone showers," I said, rolling my tongue gloatingly around the next words, "and often the girls get in together and soap up each other's glistening smooth bodies until they're covered in creamy bubbles of lather..."

Connie tried to stifle a grimace.

"... and sometimes the guys join in as well. It's amazing how quickly porn actors can get hard again, even straight after filming a sex scene like the one we just did," I twisted the knife with merciless delight. "Hell, I've known times when the shower after filming turns into some massive orgy of flesh. In fact, I bet if we went into that bathroom right now..."

"I get it!" Connie snapped.

She was angry — my job was done. I finished my drink and went back to the kitchen for a refill. I caught a glimpse of the big clock on the wall. "I have a couple of hours now until I shoot my scene with the young blonde," I said. "I will need to spend some of that time talking to her and preparing her for filming, but the rest of the time is for you," I bowed to her in a magnanimous gesture. "Would you like to ask your questions now, or would you prefer to cool down for a while?"

Connie set her glass down on a coffee table. "I'd like to ask my questions now if that's okay." I came back into the living room, but I didn't sit down. Connie settled herself on the sofa and flipped through her notebook until she found a blank page while I wandered around in aimless circles, dodging furniture.

"So how did you end up performing in the porn industry? I can't believe it was a career choice."

I smiled. "It was, actually," I said. "Working in porn was something I aspired to when I was still a teenager."

"Really?"

I nodded. "Really."

Connie made a note of that and looked back up into my eyes. "So tell me."

"My story?"

"Yes. Tell me how you got your big break – I assume there was one, right?"

I nodded. "There was," I agreed. "But my introduction to the industry was not conventional... and it's quite a long story."

Connie sat back and crossed her legs. The pen in her hand hovered over the blank page. She shrugged. "Well...?"

"The first work I got was actually as a male model," I said. "I was doing boring stud stuff – photo shoots for clothes... and in my spare time I was approaching local porn film producers. But they didn't want me. They said I was too handsome. They said I would be better suited to gay films."

"Because of your looks?"

I nodded. "The whole model thing," I shrugged. "It pissed me off."

"So what did you do?"

"I sulked," I admitted. "I had this dream of being a successful male porn actor, and no one would even let me audition. For a few months, I gave up, and then I decided to change the way I looked."

Connie was scribbling notes quickly. "Did that affect your modeling work?"

"Yeah," I said. "The agencies stopped calling."

"How did you change your look?"

"I got scruffy," I said. " I grew a short beard and a moustache. I was nineteen, so it took months. Then one night I went to a restaurant where I knew a big producer was having dinner. I wore ripped old jeans and a t-shirt."

She held up her hand to cut me off with dreary impatience. "And the producer saw you, realized you were a star in the making, and gave you the lead role in his next skin flick, right?"

"Wrong," I said. "What happened was more bizarre. When I went to the restaurant, the man I wanted to see was having dinner with his wife. The restaurant was crowded – maybe thirty people enjoying a quiet meal. I walked in, went to his table and stood there, demanding he give me an audition because I wanted to be a porn actor."

"Just like that?"

I nodded.

"In front of all of those people and his wife?"

I nodded again. "In front of everyone."

She leaned forward, suspecting there was more I hadn't yet revealed. "So what did the guy say?"

I smiled, recalling the night and the look on the producer's face when I had confronted him. "He looked me up and down and grunted. He told me that it was one thing to talk the talk, but if I wanted to be a porn actor I first had to learn how to walk the walk. More than that, he told me a porn actor was expected to perform in front of film crews. He was daring me – challenging me. I could see it in his eyes."

"So what did you do?"

"Nothing," I said. "The guy was a famous producer. All I wanted was a chance to prove myself. Then he got up from his chair and stood right in front of me. 'Can you fuck in front of a crowd, boy?' he asked me. I nodded. The truth was that I didn't know. But I wanted a chance so desperately that I told him I could."

"And he gave you the chance?"

"Yes... but not on a film set. The chance I got was right then, as we were standing in the restaurant."

Connie frowned, confused. "What do you mean?"

"I mean he stood there and told me he wanted to watch me fuck his wife. He wanted me to bend her over the restaurant table and fuck her in front of the other diners. If I got hard, and if I satisfied his wife, he would give me the chance."

"You're kidding!" Connie's voice sounded scandalized.

I wasn't. I shook my head.

Connie leaned forward. "What happened?"

I took a long gulp of my drink. "The producer's wife was a Spanish woman," I said. "She was about thirty. She had long straight black hair, flawless honey-brown skin, and exotic Mediterranean features. She was wearing one of those Spanish kind of off-the-shoulder blouses," I made crazy hand signals trying to describe how it had puffy sleeves and held together with elastic. "You know the kind?"

Connie nodded.

"Well when the producer told her to stand up, she turned to me and there was a sly taunting smile on her lips and a flash of something wicked and daring in her eyes. So I tugged her blouse down, and her breasts bounced free."

"In front of everyone?"

"In front of the whole restaurant," I confirmed.

"And what did this woman's husband do?"

"Nothing."

101

"What about the woman? What did she do?"

"She stood there. Her eyes never left my face."

Connie gasped and then asked with slow caution, "Is this story true?"

I nodded. "Every word of it," I said. "I cupped the woman's breasts and she arched her back, so I took one of her nipples in my mouth and wrapped my arm around her waist. She was wearing a long skirt, but I couldn't work out how to unfasten it," I shook my head ruefully and my smile was embarrassed. "I spent five damn minutes trying to work out how to get her fucking dress off, and all the while I'm sucking on her breasts and she's moaning and groaning with her fingers tugging at my hair.

"Meanwhile everyone in the restaurant had stopped eating and were gathering around like spectators at a boxing match. Finally, I gave up on the damn skirt. I spun the woman around and put my hand in the middle of her back. She folded forward at the waist and gripped the edge of the table. I lifted the skirt up over her waist and fucked her while she stared across the table at her husband."

"My god," Connie breathed.

"My god is right!" I said. "I had hold of this sexy woman's hips, and I was driving my cock into her like there was no tomorrow. You see, I was desperate to make an impression. I wanted to be a porn actor more than anything and I realized this was my one chance not only to start my career but also to spark a legend. So I fucked this woman so furiously that the bottle of red wine they were sharing for dinner overturned on the table and spilled into the producer's lap."

"But you got the acting job, right?" Connie asked softly.

"Yeah, I got the job... and two days later I got to fuck the producer's wife again."

"What? He made you audition again?"

I shook my head. "No... I just got to fuck his wife again... and again... and again. We ended up having an affair that lasted several months. Hell, I screwed that woman so many times I now know every Spanish swear word."

Connie had stopped writing. She was just staring up at me while I wandered in circles aimlessly about the room. For some reason, I kept circling back towards the kitchen, and I figured that meant I needed another drink.

"So... at some point you made the leap from just being a well performing actor in other people's films, to a producer yourself. Tell me how that happened."

I finished pouring my drink, dropped two cubes of ice into the glass and considered the question. "I got sick," I said.

A look of stricken horror suddenly washed over Connie's face. Her hand clamped across her mouth. "My god, you haven't got HIV... have you?"

I shook my head. "Don't be ridiculous," I said. "I got bronchitis."

"Bronchitis? That's all?"

I nodded. "That's right – but I was ill for several months, and I lost a lot of my physical condition and some weight. I also lost some of my passion for performing. That's when I decided that I needed a new level of performance creativity – I need new challenges."

Connie made some notes and then glanced up again. "And so you started producing your own films?"

"No. I started making it a condition that when I performed in other people's films, I got the chance to direct some of the scenes. I knew that if I was going to ever become a film producer I had to learn about lighting and camera angles and sound – and the things I had picked up from performing on set weren't enough. I needed practical experience, so I started shooting scenes and becoming more involved in mapping out the way a scene was going to unfold. I didn't make the leap to movie producer until just a few years ago," I said.

Connie thought for a moment. "And that's when you built the facilities in Europe."

"That's right," I said. "I wanted the whole process under one roof – the sets and the post production facilities, so I bought several acres of land in the Czech republic and spent half of all the money I had earned in building a massive house, gardens and a tennis court. A year later I had a large warehouse built that houses all the production equipment upstairs and has several interior sets on the ground level." I swallowed my drink in one gulp and Connie gave me a quizzical eye.

"Is that when you developed a drinking problem?" she looked at me pointedly.

I shook my head. "Connie, I don't have a problem drinking. It's when I stop drinking I have a problem."

She didn't smile. The woman had no sense of humor.

"Anyhow... the land I bought has a river running through it and there was some grassy marshland that I had excavated and turned into a shallow water pond. It means now that I have twenty different locations I can use for filming, all within a few miles of my production facilities... and that means I can produce quality films in an endless variety of locations and with the cost savings that come with that kind of convenience. Make sense?"

Connie nodded a grudging agreement. "Yes..." she said, "it does actually. It sounds to me like you have just taken the Hollywood model for film making and creating something similar – on a smaller scale – in Europe."

I winked. "That's exactly what I did, and Hollywood was my inspiration. The big difference is that my films don't cost a hundred million dollars to produce."

Connie bowed her head over her notebook and wrote furiously for the next few minutes. I screwed the lid tight on the whiskey bottle and filled my glass with water. I took a sip. The stuff tasted like shit – but at least it gave me a moment where I felt puffed up with virtue.

I waited until Connie finished writing before draining the rest of my drink.

(I wanted her to see me).

She looked disapproving. "Vodka is no different to whiskey," she said.

"That was water," I said. I felt cheated.

"Of course it was," she said dryly. "Now can you tell me about the health risks involved in the industry? Surely having unprotected sex with so many women is like playing Russian roulette with your life."

I smiled, and slowly unscrewed the cap off the bottle of whiskey again...

"This is a constant criticism," I said, "and to someone outside of the industry, I can understand the fear. You are right – on the surface the idea of having unprotected sex with literally thousands of partners would seem like suicidal madness," I agreed. "But... the industry isn't like that, Connie. I have regular health checks – and I never miss one. And I insist that every single actress I work with and every single actor who performs in my films produce a current medical certificate before they walk on set. I'm very strict about that – it is one of my cardinal rules that I will not break for anyone, for any reason. If an actress appears on set for filming and she cannot produce a current certificate, then she simply doesn't work. Regular health checks are mandatory in the established porn industry."

"And everyone plays by these rules, Rick?"

I shook my head. "I can't vouch for every film maker out there – I can only tell you my rules for my films. But I can tell you that every other established producer that I know has the same rule." I suddenly became animated. I waved my arms in the air like I was being attacked by a swarm of bees. "Porn actors and actresses aren't idiots, Connie. They – more than most people – understand the importance of staying healthy and being checked regularly. No actress I know would willingly take the risk of performing in a film with other actors who didn't have a clean bill of health."

"What about the age of the girls, Rick?"

Discreetly, I poured a half glass of whiskey...

"What about it?"

Connie shrugged like I should understand what she meant. "All the girls you use in your films. They all look so young. The actresses you have here today – not one of them looks over twenty-two years old – and I imagine that's the same in all your other movies as well, right?"

I nodded. "If you are asking me whether an actress needs to be young and pretty to appear in my movies, then the answer is yes," I said. "That doesn't mean that there aren't plenty of women in their thirties, forties and even fifties who still do porn. Some of the mature women do very well for themselves – they started out in the industry as pretty young things and have forged successful careers appealing to different audiences and different fetishes as they matured. Surely you've heard of a MILF?"

Connie nodded carefully. "I've heard the expression..."

"It stands for 'mother I'd like to fuck'. It's a whole sub-genre of the industry that has become huge."

"What about you?"

"What about me?" I frowned.

"Have you ever had sex with an older woman?" Connie asked. She arched an eyebrow and made her eyes wide so her expression was artless – or maybe a challenge. "Or do you just have sex with the pretty young ones?"

I thought for a moment, then titled my head and smiled mischievously. "Connie, is that an invitation?" I lowered my voice and ran my eye with speculative appreciation over the journalist's body, starting at the firm press of her breasts beneath the crisp starched blouse and finishing at her feet, thrust into high heel pumps. When my gaze returned to her face, I saw she was smiling back at me, but it was a frigid little thing without any trace of humor.

"It was a question," she said. "Just a question. It's what we journalists do. We ask a lot of them."

I sniffed at the whiskey and downed it like it was medicine. "Too bad," I shrugged. "You look like you would enjoy a good fuck. It looks like you have a sexy body going to waste." I paused, studying the effect of my words. I saw the storm clouds of Connie's anger gathering in her expression. "There are plenty of empty bedrooms here, and I have an hour or two to spare before I film the next scene. Why don't we go and spend that time together – naked."

Connie sneered, then shook her head so that her long dark hair broke and shimmered across her shoulders in a cascade. She glanced away for an instant, as though my gaze unnerved her.

"You're not my type," she said, but I sensed her sudden breathlessness, and there was emotion in her voice, like maybe she was flattered or suddenly made very nervous.

"Really?" I asked, bemused. I took another sip of whiskey and studied Connie over the rim of the glass. "Then tell me what exactly is your type?"

Connie stood up. She folded her arms, shifting her weight so that her hip swayed to one side, emphasizing the narrowness of her waist and the press of her thigh against the fabric of her skirt. She stared at me and there was an unsettled flutter behind her eyes. She lifted her chin an inch in an attempted gesture of confidence and composure.

"Older," she said, her voice lower and huskier than I had heard it before. "And wiser."

I made a face like I wasn't convinced. "No one needs to know."

She shook her head again, as though the notion was so outrageous she was horrified. "You're eight years younger than me," she explained. "I'm not some kind of a cougar or... or one of your MILFS. I don't date younger men."

"Date?" I frowned. "Connie, I never suggested we date. I suggested we fuck. I suggested we go into the bedroom and lose ourselves in each other's bodies for an hour – a mindless surrender to lust and passion with no consequences – no remorse or regrets. No strings attached. Just raw, primal sex. You and me – with no one ever to know."

Connie looked stunned, as if all of the air had been driven from her lungs. She stared at me, her face becoming pale, but her breathing becoming hectic. "I would know," she said softly.

"And so would I," I admitted. "I would have the memory, and so would you. But if you don't say yes, all you will have then is regret."

"And my self respect," she said pointedly. She smiled, but it was an unconvincing smile and she didn't try to hold it.

"I'm disappointed," I gave her my sad face. "I wanted to fuck you." I smiled again, relaxed and unruffled, almost as though I was enjoying myself.

"You want to corrupt me," she said. "And besides, I am in a relationship. I told you that and I would never do anything – "

"Bullshit," I cut her off. "Robert doesn't even exist."

Connie said nothing for a very long time, and when she did speak, her voice was soft and lacking conviction. "Yes, he does."

"No, he doesn't. You told me that story because you wanted to protect yourself from me... or maybe you didn't think you could trust yourself with me. Either way, your romance is pure fantasy."

Connie lowered her eyes and there was long, heavy silence. Her voice changed completely, it was bleak and flat, lacking any timber or resonance. "How did you know?"

I shrugged. "I just knew. I have spent a decade dealing with liars, con-men and fast-buck artists in the porn industry. They are the best bullshitters in the world, and when you spend that much time listening to liars, it's pretty easy to pick a bad one... and you're a bad one."

Chapter 10.

A catering van arrived with platters of food, and the cast and crew drifted out of the bedrooms in various states of undress.

I was hungry. I picked up a sandwich and eyed it suspiciously.

"What have you brought us?" I asked a thin young man in a grey uniform.

"Chef's specialties, the guy said vaguely. "An assortment of delicious local ingredients and produce all on fresh baked bread." He sounded like a walking talking menu.

I took the top off my sandwich and examined the filling. There was some kind of brown stuff, pureed until it was completely unrecognizable. It might have been meat – or wood. I couldn't tell. I tasted it and I still couldn't tell.

The caterers were paid, and then fled from the house like a gang of bandits on a smash-and-grab raid.

I threw the half-eaten sandwich into the trash bin and then beckoned Lily over to me. She was naked, and there were fading red smudges from fingers all over her thighs and arms. She came and stood close beside me, her eyes huge and intense.

I sensed Connie hovering somewhere behind me like a soft shadow.

"We're going to film your scene straight after lunch," I told Lily. "But before we work together I want to spend some time getting to know you. What I plan is for you and two of the other girls to be sunbathing beside the pool. I will come up out of the water and I'll get the two other actresses to kind of hold you down like you're some kind of a reluctant sacrifice for a few minutes. Then we'll do some fucking while the other two girls occupy themselves, and then come to join in the action. Okay?"

Lily nodded, staring at me with a slight scowl of concentration like she was taking it all in. "That sounds fab." She sounded breathless.

I smiled. "Well it's not the 'The Godfather'," I shrugged, "but then witty dialogue and complex plots aren't the kind of thing you find in porn."

The girl nodded. I doubted if she'd ever even heard of 'The Godfather', let alone understood a word I had said about dialogue and plots. But she did have a great pair of tits.

"I've... I've never had anyone as big as you," Lily said softly and a little frown of concern creased her face. "Will you be gentle?"

"As a lamb," I said and then shook my head. "Don't worry about any of that. We will spend ten minutes together in the bedroom before we start to film. Just to make sure you're comfortable."

"That would be fab!" she said again. The kid had a limited vocabulary, but she *really did* have a great pair of tits.

"Now tell me about yourself," I asked. "What made you decide to get involved in this industry?"

She shrugged her shoulders, which made those magnificent pneumatic breasts move enticingly. "Johnny introduced me to the industry," she said in a bright cheerful voice. "I was learning to be a hairdresser. One day, Johnny came in for a haircut, and we just started talking. The next thing I know, he invited me to appear in one of his films."

"Johnny? You mean John Bellamy?"

Lily nodded.

"And you just turned up on a film set one day and started in porn?"

Lily nodded again, but this time she smiled as well. "The first scene I did was a gang-bang with four guys," she said. "Johnny thought it was best if I dived right in," she giggled.

I smiled. "Hooray for Johnny," I said with dry sarcasm. "What a guy – always a gentleman, and always thinking of others first."

"He likes it when I call him big daddy," Lily leaned close and confided in a whisper.

I turned my head, glanced at Connie with revolting dismay. My lip was curled into a distasteful sneer, my eyes wide and startled. Connie's expression mirrored my own. I dropped my voice so that she alone could hear. "And you think I'm a creep," I whispered.

"You are a creep," she whispered back tartly but there was a smile on the end of her lips. Just a very little one.

I turned back to Lily. "Do you miss hairdressing?"

She shook her head, and I swear I heard something inside that big empty space rattle.

"Not at all," Lily piped softly. "I love doing porn movies," she enthused. "I want to be a star. That's why Johnny sent me to you," she clutched at my arm and drew herself closer. She looked up

113

into my face with misguided adoration. "You're the biggest name in the whole porn world, Rick Cassidy. Johnny told me that if I fuck you, it could make my career." She did a jiggly, bouncy thing on her tiptoes, which I interpreted as being enthusiasm.

Her breasts were rubbing against my chest, and I could feel the hard stub of her nipples through the fabric of my shirt. They moved like they had a life of their own. She was flirting with me.

"Are you an L.A. girl?" I looked down into her eyes.

Lily shook her head again. "I'm from New Jersey originally," she said. "I moved to Los Angeles with my mother about four years ago."

"You like it here?"

"Sure," Lily smiled. She had very white teeth – made whiter by the flawlessness of her summer tan. "What's not to like?"

I made a face. "A lot of people like New Jersey," I said.

Lily's face became a pout. "Not me," she said. "Not after..." She stopped. It was a painful memory. "... My father was killed in a car accident. He got caught up in the middle of a police chase. The guy had robbed a convenience store. He crashed into my father's car as he was driving home from work. After... after everything, my mom decided we needed a fresh start."

"And she chose to bring you to L.A.?"

Lily's face brightened, and I got the feeling she wasn't the kind of deep thinker who would dwell on something like sadness for very long. She

114

nodded. "Mom's moving back to New Jersey in the winter," she said. "She misses family."

"But you're not, right?"

"Right," she smiled. "I'm staying here."

"To make a name for yourself in porn?"

"Uhuh," Lily's eyes became wider. Her hand drifted up my arm and I could feel the press of her fingers through my shirt like she was massaging my bicep. "Johnny thinks I have what it takes."

I smiled thinly. "What about your mother?"

Lily furrowed her brow. "What about her?"

"Does she know you are making porn films?"

Lily shook her head. "I don't live with her anymore," she said. "I live with Johnny." She brightened suddenly. "He bought me a car and a horse!"

"Of course he did," I muttered dryly. I disentangled myself from the girl, and stole a glance over my shoulder where the big clock was ticking away the afternoon. "I want to shoot this scene in an hour," I said. "So why don't you grab yourself a bite to eat and then meet me in the main bedroom in about twenty minutes time. We'll make sure tab 'A' fits into slot 'B' before the cameras start rolling."

"That would be fab!" Lily giggled and jiggled.

Chapter 11.

I left Connie hovering over a platter of sandwiches and drifted down the hallway into the main bedroom. Lily was lying naked on the bed, waiting for me. She looked sensational. The contrast of her brown skin set against the crisp white sheets took my breath away.

"We only have ten or so minutes," I explained. "I just want to make sure you're going to be comfortable, Lily. I don't want to get on set and have you screaming before I want you to scream," I smiled.

Lily nodded. "I've been fingering myself while I was waiting for you," she said. "I'm pretty wet down there. And kind of tingly."

I went to the edge of the bed. I unfastened my jeans, drew down the zipper. My cock sprang out, half-hard. Lily sat upright on the bed with a look of awe and wonder on her face, as though maybe she'd seen a UFO.

"God," she whispered. "It's not natural."

She reached out tentatively and touched my shaft with the tip of one finger. She giggled. "It's so big, and it's getting even bigger."

She tried to wrap her hand around me, then opened her mouth as wide as she could and took the tip of me between her lips. She danced her fingers along my length like she was playing a trumpet. I felt my erection thicken. My body clenched my shaft pulsed and leapt.

Lily stopped giggling. Her eyes became big and serious. She gulped the first few inches of me into her mouth and held me there with a frown of concentration on her brow.

I reached down and drew my hand from her shoulder, down across her breasts. Lily was making grunting gasping sounds. She eased my cock from her mouth and swirled her tongue around the swollen end of me.

"That will do," I said. "Let's try you on your hands and knees first." I saw the waver of doubt in her eyes, the slight twist of her mouth. She nodded.

Lily knelt on the bed and braced herself with her knees wide apart. She collapsed her arms so that her head was lowered, her face pressed against the pillow. I positioned myself behind her and set the end of my cock against the flared glistening lips of her sex.

"I'll be gentle," I promised, and then eased just the first couple of inches of myself inside the tight gripping depths of the girl's body.

"Ooooh," Lily gasped. She started breathing in short ragged pants and I felt her undulate her hips as though to accommodate me. I saw her hands clench into fists. "You're so big," she groaned.

I leaned into her carefully, until half my length had disappeared into her pussy. Lily sucked in a sudden hiss of breath and there was a moment where I felt her body seize and then spasm. She hoisted herself up onto her arms, and turned her head to glance over her shoulder at me. There was hectic color splashed across her face and her lips were drawn back into a grimace of pain and pleasure. "Is that it? Are you all the way in?"

I shook my head. "Just a little further," I said.

She nodded and then bit her bottom lip. "Give it to me."

I gripped Lily's hips, splayed my fingers wide to hold her body still and slid myself all the way inside her pussy.

Lily started to shudder. Her arms trembled, and the color seemed to drain away from her face. Her mouth fell wide open, and her eyes rolled up. She started shaking her head from side to side, long blonde hair swishing across her back. "Fuck!" she sobbed.

"Are you okay?" I asked.

Lily nodded. She began to rock and sway her body gently from side to side. I held myself still within her until she groaned and then seemed to turn to jelly. Suddenly the tension went from her. I drew myself back and then drove forward again.

"Are you okay?" I asked again.

Lily nodded.

Slowly, we worked our bodies into a gentle rhythm until Lily stopped gasping for breath and started moaning with pleasure. My shaft was slick and glistening with the juices from her pussy, sliding deep inside her and being gripped in the vice-like tightness of her body.

"Are you still okay?"

"Yes," Lily said breathlessly. I nodded, and then stepped back from her.

Lily collapsed on the bed, legs wide apart, arms splayed across the mattress so that she looked like she'd fallen from a tall building and hit a pavement. I pulled on my jeans and sat on the edge of the bed. Lily turned her head to look at me.

"Fuck..." she said again.

I brushed a loose tendril of golden hair away from her forehead with a tender touch. "Do you still want to film this scene with me?" I asked.

Lily made a brave little face and nodded. "That would be fab," she whispered.

Chapter 12.

It was two o'clock before we were ready for filming. Getting the three girls organized was like herding cats — they wandered from room to room without any sense of urgency until I started shouting. Then things happened quickly.

I assembled everyone involved in the scene outside by the pool, with Connie standing discreetly in the background. Victor, Roland and the two girls they had performed with that morning had disappeared into the city, so the house had an almost abandoned feel to it.

"Okay, this is how it's going to go down," I clapped my hands to get everyone's attention. "Kate and Kelly, I need you two girls to work with Lily on this scene. She doesn't have a lot of experience, and so I need you girls to make her look good."

The two actresses were experienced. I had worked with Kate several times back when I was performing in films for other people. Kelly was one of my regular actresses who I had first met in Prague. We had filmed a couple of scenes together in the last twelve months, and she had flown out from Europe for this shoot with the other girls.

"Lily, honey, just be natural," I insisted. "They don't hand out academy awards for porn films, so you can forget about acting for this scene. I just want you to be you, and I want your reactions to be genuine. Let yourself go, and *feel* what's happening as the scene develops. Do you understand me?"

Lily nodded her head. Her eyes were huge and solemn, and I had a sense that she was taking this all very seriously.

"If you really want to put in a memorable performance, then you must remember not to perform. The camera is going to love you," I reached out, put my finger under her chin and lifted her face so that she was looking into my eyes and could see the sincerity of my words. "Just relax and be yourself. When the sex starts I want you to be instinctive. Work with me, and everything will be fine."

Lily nodded again. I could feel her trembling with nerves.

"We'll start the scene with the three girls sunbathing together beside the pool. Let's get some sex going between you all — just do what comes naturally for the first few minutes. After you girls are comfortable and into each other, I am going to emerge from the pool." I looked hard at Kate and Kelly and pointed a finger at them both. "That will be your cue. I want you girls to kind of hold Lily down for me to fuck. Understand?"

The girls understood.

"Once Lily and I get started, you two girls just join in, and maybe a little bit of sexy action between you two on the side would be good."

I couldn't make it simpler. I turned to my camera guys, and my voice became harder and more serious. "Make sure you get plenty of close up action between the girls as the scene opens, okay? I will be watching from in the pool. When I think we've got enough footage I'm going to give you a cue and then I'll duck under the surface. Walter, when you see me go under, I want you to pan out wide from the girls to get a shot of the pool in the background. About twenty seconds later I'm going to rise up from out of the pool and I want that shot with the girls in the foreground and me coming up out of the water in the background." I did all crazy kind of things with my hands to explain the scene in gestures. The cameramen nodded and we broke apart and went to our positions like a football huddle after the quarterback has called the play.

The water was fucking freezing!

I stood waist deep in the swimming pool with my arms folded across my chest, shivering with cold. I could feel my testicles trying to climb up inside my body, looking for a warm place to hide. I clenched my jaw and my teeth chattered together, while on the warm decking, the three girls spread themselves out naked on top of thick fluffy beach towels. The camera guys got into position, careful to avoid their shadows from the afternoon sun stretching across the setting.

"Action!" I shuddered. I prayed the girls would lunge at each other in a sex-maddened frenzy, because if I stayed in this pool for too long, I was sure my cock would snap off. I reached down and felt around. Everything was still there, just shrunken and shriveled. By the time I climbed out of this fucking pool, I was going to look like a eunuch.

"Action," I called again. My voice squeaked.

Not for the first time, I was grateful to be working with experienced actresses. Kate raised herself up on her elbows and glanced with hungry eyes over Lily's naked body. I had the young girl sandwiched between my two actresses, and as Kate's eyes roamed over the firm contours of young Lily's nakedness, she shook her long blonde hair out and then rolled onto her side.

"You are very sexy," Kate said in a thick German accent. Lily's eyes fluttered open and Kate lowered her face and kissed Lily sensually on the lips.

On the other side of her, Kelly produced a small bottle of oil and began to massage Lily's thighs so that they glistened in the sunlight. Kelly was a dark-haired beauty, and the contrast of the two girls caressing different parts of Lily's body would look good on camera.

With Lily laying submissively on her back, Kate finally broke the kiss. Her mouth hunted the young girl's neck while her hands swept over her breasts, pinching and rubbing her nipples. She eased herself over where Lily lay so that one of her breasts hung close to the girl's lips. Lily's mouth opened instinctively and Kate closed her eyes and groaned as Lily sucked one of the blonde's nipples into her mouth.

"Fingers," I called to Kelly, directing the scene from the pool. "Get your fingers inside her pussy."

Lily raised her knees and dug her tiny heels into the towel. Her thighs fell open and Kelly poured lotion into her cupped hand, and then spread the oil across the young girl's abdomen, working her fingers in slow lazy circles until they were brushing the pouting lips of Lily's shaved sex. Kelly's fingers were demanding. She rubbed

123

Lily's clit with her thumb and then reached inside the girl.

Lily moaned. She lifted her hips up off the towel, rocking them from side to side as Kelly's probing and teasing touch became more insistent.

Kelly got up onto her hands and knees, and one of the cameramen hovered close behind her, shooting the action from between the dark haired girl's parted knees.

"Good," I said, visualizing the view through the lens in my mind's eye. "Now go down on her, Kelly."

Kate pulled the girl's legs wider apart and Kelly crawled around and buried her face in Lily's glistening sex. I heard young Lily suck in a deep hissing breath of ecstasy, and then one of her hands appeared, slid from Kate's breast and seized the hair at the back of Kelly's head to hold her tight between her thighs.

"Okay, Walter," I said at last. "Pan back and get ready for that wide shot."

I ducked my head below the surface.

Fuck!

(the water was freezing).

I think I held my breath – or maybe the shocking cold just seized the oxygen in my lungs. I counted slowly to ten, and then more quickly to twenty, and then rose slowly up out of the water, with my hair plastered flat against my skull, water streaming into my eyes and running down my chest as I waded to the edge of the pool where the girls were entwined.

I heaved myself out of the pool. There was a sharp pain in my chest and I realized my lungs had kicked in and I was breathing again. I stood over the girls, dripping wet, gazing down upon this delicious banquet of beauty like it was the first time I had ever seen such a thing in my life, and I prayed to God that one of the guys was filming me from the waist up.

Kate turned her head, looked up at me with an admiring gaze. She hooded her eyes invitingly. Her breast slipped from between Lily's sucking lips and she crawled over to me in one of those erotic hip-swaying feline movements that only women know how to do.

"Suck me," I whispered.

Kate cupped her hands around me and took my shaft into the hot heat of her mouth. I closed my eyes, threw my head back, and felt a wash of afternoon sunshine across my face.

I felt Kate's tongue fluttering and coaxing along the underside of my cock as her lips wrapped tight around my length and she drew them back and forth with hungry lunges.

I reached down and splayed my fingers into her blonde, tousled hair, and then braced my legs.

This was another advantage of working with girls I was familiar with – they knew me – and they knew what I needed. Kate became instantly passive, the tension melted from her body, and I felt her throat relax. I pumped myself back and forth, pushing from my hips, and using her mouth like it was a pussy to get myself hard.

Kate had her eyes closed. I stared passed her and suddenly saw Connie standing quietly in the shade of the house. She was watching me, her gaze unwavering, her expression fathomless. Our eyes locked for an instant, and then I felt a rush of warm blood around my groin as my cock suddenly filled and became hard. Kate made a gasping sound that came from deep inside her chest and my attention flicked back to the scene unfolding before me.

Kate's eyes were open now, watering. I eased my hardness from between her lips and she choked a ragged breath of relief and then licked her puffy swollen lips. I reached down for her and lifted her to her feet. I kissed her with sudden urgency, wrapping one arm around her tiny waist and pulling her hard against me. Her hand stroked me as we embraced and she moaned into my mouth with a sound of raw and genuine desire. I slid my hand down over her bottom and she shuffled her feet apart as my fingers explored her sex. She tilted her pelvis to open herself to me and then wrapped a desperate arm around my neck as I touched the lips of her pussy. Her teeth bit into my lip. She was panting. I could feel the movement of her body and the press of her breasts with every frantic breath. The tip of my finger inched inside her and she came up onto her tiptoes, her body strained in anticipation.

"Fuck me," she breathed, not loud enough for the microphone on the camera.

I turned her around and folded her forward at the waist. I rubbed the swollen head of my shaft against the moistness of her and then pushed myself inside. Kate groaned aloud and then pushed herself back onto me so that the full length of my cock filled her entirely. I reached for her dangling arms and grasped them, pulling them behind her back to hold her still before filling her with another thrust.

One of the cameramen swung in and positioned himself in front of where Kate stood, to capture the satisfied delight on her face and the sway of her breasts as I began to fuck her with a slow steady rhythm.

For a moment Lily and Kelly were forgotten as I concentrated on sliding my cock in and out Kate's wet pussy with long slow deliberate strokes so that each moment could be captured in close up. But Kate wasn't acting.

Her legs were trembling and the grip of her pussy pulsed and vibrated with lustful desire. Her mouth was open, her eyes screwed tightly shut, and the only sound was the slap of flesh as our bodies slammed together with increasing frantic tempo.

Kate hung her head, her body going loose and soft. I let her arms go and reached around her with my fingers to rub her clit. Her knees buckled and she swayed giddily forward. "Oh, fuck, yes," she gasped.

Kelly lifted her face from between Lily's spread legs and licked her juice-covered lips. She spun around and crawled to where Kate was bent over. She looked up into my eyes as though seeking permission, and then craned her neck forward and her tongue flicked out across my fingertips. I moved my hand and Kelly reached out with her mouth and planted her lips against Kate's clit as the shaft of my cock slid into her pussy.

Kate groaned again and both cameras came in at different angles to shoot the sequence. I felt

Kate's pussy begin to spasm. I gave one last thrust of my hips and then eased myself from her. She moaned and shot me a glance of frustration from over her shoulder. I ignored her and took a step back. Kelly reached for my cock with her hand, and licked Kate's glistening juices from my shaft like she had been presented with a delicious treat to savor.

My cock felt rock hard. It twitched and gripped as Kelly's magical tongue flickered and her lips nibbled. Beyond where she knelt, Lily lay spread out on the towel, one hand between her thighs, her fingers wiggling dexterously.

I hoped she was wet and ready...

My cock came from Kelly's mouth reluctantly and she gave me a petulant little pout with her lips. I nodded in Lily's direction and the two girls understood. They turned away from me and crawled across the towels to where Lily lay. Each girl took a leg, spreading them wide apart. Lily's eyes flicked open at their touch and then settled on my face. She let out a shuddering, anxious breath and trapped her lip between her teeth.

"Hold her down," I said for the cameras. "I want to give her a fuck she will never forget."

(Hollywood this ain't).

The two women covered Lily with their mouths and roaming hands like devouring vampires feasting on willing flesh. I sank to my knees between the girl's parted thighs and held her legs against my sides. My cock twitched in the air, leaping from my crotch as I clenched the muscles in my body. Kate reached between us and guided my shaft until it was poised and pressing gently against her sex.

I slid forward slowly. The first two inches of me nudged inside Lily's pussy. She arched up like someone doing stomach crunches and watched with wide open eyes as my cock disappeared inside her. Kate fisted one hand in Lily's hair and attacked her mouth with a passionate kiss.

I kept pressing my weight forward until Lily began to gasp and gulp ragged breaths. The lips of her pussy were flared wide open, stretched tight around the ridged length of my shaft. Kelly laid her cheek on Lily's abdomen so that her mouth was just an inch away from where our bodies connected. She lashed out with her tongue and teased Lily's pulsing clit.

I waited until Walter was able to move the camera. He came and stood behind me, filming down from over my shoulder. I slid the last inches of me into Lily's pussy and let out a long deep groan of blissful satisfaction.

"You're so fucking tight," I grunted, knowing the words would pick up clearly in the effects mike. "Your pussy is amazing."

Walter backed away to get a different angle and Kate got to her feet and took his place. She dropped to her knees and wrapped one of her hands around my waist, grinding her pelvis against me.

"Fuck her, baby," she whispered in my ear. "Give her the fuck she needs."

I began to drive my cock in and out of Lily's pussy. She was gasping with every deep stroke, swishing her head from side to side. Her mouth was wide open, her eyes wrenched tightly shut. Each time I drew back, until just the tip of me remained inside, she made a choking plea for more. When we had filmed for several minutes, I ordered Lily up onto her hands and knees. Reflected shards of glinting light bounced off the blue water in the swimming pool and refracted on Lily's tanned body like a hundred tiny mirrors. It caught the highlights of color in her hair and made it shimmer. The teenager turned her head, glanced back over her shoulder at me and slowly opened her glazed eyed. She smiled, then wiggled her hips and tilted her pelvis at a saucy angle in invitation.

I slowly stroked my cock, acting aroused and gazing upon her lithe firm body with a look that I hoped was one of desire.

Kate knelt beside the pool and fondled Lily's breasts with the palms of her hands.

"Fuck me, stud," Lily said. "Now I've had a taste, I'm begging you for more."

I didn't look, but I could imagine Connie rolling her eyes and gagging.

I drew the moment out. I stood back, enjoying the sight of the two blonde girls on their knees together, and took the opportunity to thrust myself back inside Kelly's ever-willing mouth. She sucked me with ravenous slurping sounds of desire and coated the entire length of my shaft with the wetness of her kisses.

Timing in this business is everything. I wanted the cameras to get a couple of minutes of footage before we set up for the final fuck and come shot. As Kelly tried to force me all the way down her throat, I waited patiently until Walter was finally in position.

I knelt down behind Lily and seized her hips. She was so tiny, so slim, my hands looked like baseball mitts as my fingers dug into the firm tanned flesh of her ass. She seemed to sense what was about to happen. Suddenly her head sunk between her shoulders and a ripple of tense expectation tightened through her body.

My cock slid all the way inside Lily in one long stroke that drove the breath explosively from her lungs in a shuddering gasp and her body came instantly alive under the touch of my fingers, trembling and thrilling.

"You fuck me so fab," she sighed. The joints of her elbows collapsed and she slumped forward, so that her forehead brushed against the towel. I began to drive myself in and out of her tight pussy and Lily swayed her body to meet my lunges. The air filled with the sounds and scents of sex: the rasps of harsh breathing, the undulating moans and groans of desire.

I could feel the first stir of a familiar tingling deep in the pit of my guts and tiny flickering sparks of fire began to ignite themselves along the length of my shaft. I felt myself swell to impossible size and knew that I was just moments away from exploding.

The cameramen sensed it too.

So did Kate and Kelly.

The two girls knelt in expectation, anticipating the come shot.

Lily didn't.

(Fucking amateurs!)

"I want to ride you," she said so that not only the cameras heard it, but probably the neighbors as well. "I want to sit on top of your big hard cock."

I froze for an instant of dismay.

Fuck!

I slid my cock from between her legs and rolled onto my back, keeping the simmer of my sudden frustrated temper hidden behind my eyes. Lily spun in a dancer's pirouette and then stood over me, one hand between her legs, languidly teasing her sex. Her eyes were enormous in her young blonde face. She licked her lips and then took the deep kind of breath that someone takes before they plunge into an ice bath.

She lowered herself down, bending at the knees, her back straight, her mouth so wide open it seemed unhinged from her jaw. She wrapped delicate fingers around the base of my cock and we all watched with a hypnotic kind of fascination as she took every inch of me inside herself.

For long moments she didn't move – she sat, full with the heat of me, and her eyes became misty and distant. Kate reached across our bodies and flicked her fingers across Lily's swollen clit. Slowly Lily began to move, rising up, straining the muscles in her calves and thighs and then dropping down again and rocking her hips like my cock was a child's fairground ride.

I closed my eyes and gritted my teeth. This was not what I had planned. This had the promise of a complete disaster. The reason come shots are never filmed in this position is because it's too damned hard to get the timing right. With the girl bouncing up and down on an actor's cock, the moment of his release had to be judged perfectly. Too soon, and you end up with the actress needing to perform five minutes of hand job action before the guy finally gets off. Too late, and you end up with no visible come shot at all.

Fucking amateurs!

"I'm going to come," I growled at last.

Lily had her head thrown back, her eyes shut. She was cupping her breasts in her hands as they bounced with impossible perfection. She heard my voice and slid herself off my cock.

Panic. Confusion.

Lily squealed.

I opened my eyes, blinked in the harsh glare of sunlight, and then focused. Lily was kneeling astride me with her tiny hand expertly stroking the top of my cock. It was swollen and engorged – an instant away from erupting.

"This is for you!" Lily's voice chirped. Kate and Kelly lunged forward open-mouthed at the precise moment where I lost the last shreds of my restraint. My orgasm gushed, arching into the air between the actresses' faces. It splashed on their tongues and into their mouths. It spattered across Lily's sweat-glistening breasts.

It looked spectacular.

I lay prone, sucking in huge lungfulls of air as the moment of rapture faded and then dissolved. I sensed my two cameramen peeling away from the action and just a minute later they stopped filming.

"Tell me you got that," I pleaded.

Walter came over and crouched beside where I lay. He was smiling. "Every instant of it," he smiled.

I sat up. Lily was still sitting astride my hips. There was an expression of satisfaction and triumph spreading softly across her lips. "Did I do good?"

Chapter 13.

I was sweating heavily: it trickled down my back, glistened across my chest and burned at my eyes. I stood naked in the cool shade of the kitchen for just long enough to pour three fingers of whiskey, and then I carried the glass with me into the living room where Connie was pacing with agitation. There was a dark flush of color under her cheeks.

"What did you think?" I asked. I dragged the back of my hand across my brow.

"Interesting," Connie's voice was reedy. She was looking into my eyes, but I sensed her distraction. We were standing close. Connie took a small step back and I caught the briefest flicker of her gaze as it dropped to where my cock hung, still half-hard after filming. "You certainly put everything into your performance."

I raised an eyebrow. "You mean the different positions?"

"That," she said, "and the energy you bring."

"Is that a compliment?" I wasn't sure.

Connie's smile twisted a little. "It was a comment."

"You mean a criticism."

"No. I mean a comment," she said. "Nothing more."

I closed the space between us with a single step until we were standing just a few inches apart. Connie sucked in a sudden disconcerted breath, as if it might be the last one she ever took. I stared down into her eyes and her gaze was nervous and hectic.

"Did watching the scene turn you on?" my voice lowered, becoming intimate.

She said nothing. I could see her lower lip quivering. She tried to avert her eyes, but there was nowhere else to look.

Except down at my cock.

"Did you get aroused, watching me fuck those girls?"

"No," she told a breathless little lie. "Not at all."

I stepped back, a knowing smile on my lips. "That's a shame," I said. "Because while I was fucking Lily, I was thinking about you, Connie. I was fantasizing about how nice it would be to slowly undress you, remove your bra and panties and then slowly cover your body with soft wet kisses while you writhed beneath me."

Connie looked shocked... or maybe it was an expression of something more feminine and primal. "Is that so?" she flustered, her composure shaking.

"Yes, it is," I smiled wolfishly. "I was fantasizing about having sex with you – away from the cameras, away from the actresses who do this for a living. I was thinking about how erotic it would be to take you to bed and taste your pussy." As I spoke, my cock began to harden again. "I hope that doesn't offend you. I'm sure you are the focus of a lot of men's fantasies."

Connie didn't answer. She took an uncertain step aside, and as she did, her eyes drifted distractedly downwards...

"Maybe you should be concentrating more on your job," she offered feebly.

I smiled. "Maybe I've decided to make it my job to take you to bed."

She laughed, but the sound of it rattled in her throat, hollow and unconvincing. She shook her head and folded her arms across her chest. "Forget it," she said off-balance. "You're not my type of man."

I arched an eyebrow. "Type? What type of man am I?"

Connie's features suddenly became composed. Her eyes fixed on mine, cold and appraising. "You're a cobra," she said softly. "A big, beautiful, but very dangerous cobra. You weave and hypnotize, Rick Cassidy... you lure your targets with your looks and charm and your physique..."

"And then...?"

"And then you devour them."

There was a long moment of silence, and then I smiled lazily. "Wouldn't you like to be eaten, Connie?" my voice dropped to a sexy whisper. I reached out and touched her shoulder with the tips of my fingers. I could feel her body tremble while the double entendre hung in the air.

Connie stiffened and shook her head, but she didn't flinch away. "Not because I'm mesmerized," she insisted softly. "I don't do casual sex... and if I ever did, it would be with my eyes wide open – not under the spell of a man like you."

And that was that...

Chapter 14.

"I need a shower," I decided. "Make yourself comfortable, okay?"

I headed down the hallway to the bathroom. I drained the whiskey and left the empty glass on a side-table. I could hear the sound of the shower running from behind the closed bathroom door. I stepped into the room, into billowing clouds of soft hazy steam.

Kate was sitting on the edge of the bathroom vanity, her back against the cold tiles of the wall, her legs folded and spread wide, heels resting on the lip of the wooden counter. Lily was crouched on her knees between the actress's legs. She had her face nestled between the tall tanned blonde's thighs. Kate had her eyes closed and she was breathing loudly. I pushed the door closed behind me. The shadowy shape of Kelly was standing behind the frosted glass of the shower screen. I could see the fractured patterns of her as she ran a lather of suds over her breasts.

I didn't move.

Lily's tongue was lapping at the folds of Kate's sex with single-minded dedication. Her body rocked gently with every swipe of her tongue, and Kate's breathing altered in tone and intensity, becoming more hectic and irregular.

Lily had one hand between her own legs, cupping her sex with her palm as two of her fingers glided in and out of her pussy. I felt my cock begin to firm as if it had a mind and a will of its own.

138

"Very nice," I said. "I could watch you girls for hours."

Kate opened her eyes and gazed at me with a lost dreamy expression soft on her lips. Lily glanced over her shoulder at me. She saw my cock harden and rise and she giggled. "We can always make room for you, Rick," she said in a sultry voice. "I know there's room in my pussy for you, and I bet Katie would like the same thing too."

I smiled. The door to the shower screen slid open a few inches and a slender tanned forearm appeared through the cloud of steam. The fingers of the hand crooked into a beckoning gesture, and I heard Kelly's husky voice above the hiss of the water. "I'm in here all alone and wet as hell," she invited.

I lolled elegantly against the wall, folded my arms and crossed my ankles. "I am just a spectator, girls," I said. "I don't want to interrupt the fun."

The shower cut off abruptly and Kelly came from behind the frosted door. Her skin was pink and dewy. Her hair was pulled back into a ponytail that swished across her shoulder blades as she wrapped herself in a big white fluffy towel. She went to the vanity and swiped her palm across the glass until she could see her reflection. She bent provocatively closer and my eyes were drawn to the swell and press of her bottom through the material. She was doing it on purpose, of course. She made a pantomime of inspecting her reflection with a critical eye, and then stepped back a pace and lifted one foot to set it on the edge of the counter. The folds of the big towel fell open like a theatre curtain and I could see the fresh smooth shaved mound of her sex. She was doing this on purpose too. She smiled at me.

"You like my pussy, Rick? We fuck, yes?"

I wavered. My common sense was saying 'no', but my cock was saying 'yes'. I felt the clutch of my reaction and it made my shaft swell into hardness.

"Not today, Kelly," I said. I looked down at myself. "I need to save my energy."

The dark haired girl laughed with a mocking throaty chuckle. She reached out for my cock and took me in her hand. Her fingers were soft, gentle but insistent. She stroked my shaft slowly. "That too bad," she mangled the sentence. "Can I give him little kiss?"

She didn't wait for an answer. She dropped to her knees and opened her mouth wide. I could feel her hot breath tingling against my skin. I looked down. Her eyes were dark and slanted seductively. She reached out with the tip of her tongue and teased me with flicking tender touches.

"That's not a kiss," I said. "You're trying to arouse me."

Kelly's expression became a feigned mask of innocence, then she leaned forward, closed her eyes, and took me deep into her mouth.

I screwed my eyes shut and threw back my head, smacking the back of my skull against the wall. The pain splintered down my neck, down my spine... and then somehow dissolved at the level of my waist where Kelly's skilled mouth was generating very different sensations.

I felt my hands clench into fists at my sides and a tension crept into my body, starting at my toes and spreading like a slow burning fire.

"You like, Rick?" Kelly slid my cock from her mouth to ask the question, looking up into my face. Her hand was gently stroking me, her fingers finding every sensitive spot and massaging with infinite skill.

"I do like," I opened my eyes. "But I don't think I can give you what you want."

Kelly smiled seductively. "I just want this," she gently squeezed my cock, "for ten minutes, Rick."

"I don't think that's a good idea, Kelly."

She pouted and stood up. She ran the flat of her hand across the muscles of my chest and then slid the tip of one of her fingers into my mouth. "It is good idea, Rick," she reassured me. There was a sultry heat in her eyes. I felt her hand tight around the base of my cock. "And it would be a shame to waste this, yes? He is very hard."

A guy can only take so much.

I nodded. Kelly's grin became winning. She kissed me fiercely and I felt her tongue slide inside my mouth as she crushed herself against me. My hands slid down the curves and contours of her body and cupped the cheeks of her bottom. Kelly moaned into my mouth and rocked her hips from side to side, then turned within my arms so that she was facing away from me. My cock pressed hard between the cheeks of her butt. She reached behind her and took my shaft in her hand, leading me across to the long bathroom vanity counter like I was on a leash.

Kelly bent forward at the waist and spread her legs wide. She had her elbows propped on the vanity, staring at her own reflection in the mirror right before her. I stepped up behind her and slid my cock into her pussy.

It was fascinating to watch the play of emotions on the woman's face as I fucked her. The soft smile of deep satisfaction she wore as I entered her hung on her lips for just a few moments before her entire expression dissolved and became something else. Her eyes screwed shut, her lips parted slightly and the look on her face became one of concentration. I clung to her hips while holding her steady against the impact of each thrust, staring at our reflection in the mirror and enchanted by the way her breasts swayed in response to the rising urgent drive of my hips.

Kelly's breathing became deeper and more uncertain. Tiny misted clouds of her breath fogged the mirror. Beside us, Kate had turned her head to watch. Her eyes were glazed with her own arousal. She pulled Lily's face tight against her pussy and mashed her sex against the young girl's mouth.

"Fuck her, Rick," Kate breathed. Her back was arched, the muscles along the side of her neck drawn tense. She was close to coming against Lily's soft lips.

I could feel myself beginning to thrill. It wasn't an urgent rush born from the *need* to come – it was an instinctive physical function, the sensations created by the tight gripping pulse of the pussy I was enveloped within. I felt a vague

142

tightening of the muscles across my back and shoulders and then the slow burn of strain ignited in my thighs.

It was just a matter of time.

"Harder!" Kelly grunted. Her face was twisted into a rictus of ecstasy. She was panting now, each breath sounding like an effort. "I am so close!"

Once a man reaches the point where his body becomes overwhelmed with sensation, it's very hard to detour from the inevitable moment of eruption. I was at that point now, where the urge to come was rising up within me — and I didn't want to. In the back of my mind was the overriding demand of my profession — I needed to film two more scenes the following day and they counted for nothing if the come shot at the end of scene was less than spectacular. As much as I wanted to fill Kelly's pussy and experience that explosive moment of release, I simply couldn't afford to.

"Seventeen times eight is..." I began doing mental arithmetic to distract myself. No matter how willing the body is, it just won't work if the mind is distracted. I clenched my jaw, gritted my teeth and spent the next few minutes calculating impossibly complex math problems in my mind while, on the end of my cock, Kelly thrashed and squealed and ground her body until she finally orgasmed and went limp as a ragdoll.

Kelly dissolved into a trembling quivering gasping mound of flesh, slumped over the bathroom vanity. I staggered away. My breath was sawing in my throat, my lungs heaving like a

143

bellows. I was streaming sweat while my cock throbbed and pulsed like it was tapping out a Morse code message of distress.

For long moments, there was nothing but heavy silence ripped apart by the sound of ragged breathing. Kate had come also. She sat spent on the vanity counter, gently fondling her own breasts in the afterglow of her orgasm.

"Do you want me to finish you off, Ricky?"

It was Lily. She had Kate's glistening juices on her lips and chin. She looked up at me with a willing eagerness to please in her eyes and reached out her hand towards me.

"No," I said. "Thank you for the offer."

I knew that even the slightest touch would flick the trigger of my own release. I held up my hands, palms out as though fending off an attacker. "Don't come any closer."

Lily giggled, and my sensitive reluctance was like waving a red flag at a bull. Lily came towards me with a mischievous glint of menace sparkling in her eyes. "Aww, you can't leave that big thing just hanging there like that, Rick. Look at him. He's all swollen and angry. Let me make him better for you," she crooned.

"No. Thank you," I said again. Kate stirred to life. She gazed at me through sleepy, dreamy eyes and roused herself. She slid off the long vanity counter like a crocodile sliding off a riverbank and hunted towards me. She was smiling a predatory smile.

"Back off," I warned. I was smiling, but it was a fixed smile. The girls thought my predicament was amusing, but this was no laughing matter. I

144

covered my crotch with both hands and backed myself into a corner. "I don't need your help," I pleaded.

The girls made one last effort, tugging at my arms and licking their lips with lewd, lust-filled grins. I swatted their hands away and dashed for the open shower door.

I swung the frosted door of the shower closed and braced it shut with one hand. The girls threw themselves against the glass in fits of giggles. I had only one hand free to turn the shower on.

Hot or cold?

The water was fucking freezing!

I felt the icy blast of cold water smack against my chest and I gasped with the sudden shock of it. I ducked my head under the gush, and watched my erection shrivel.

Cured.

Chapter 15.

It was getting dark. The sun was sinking in the distance and the city was beginning to light up in screaming bright neon. I stared down into the valley, watching the winking lights and the thick streams of distant traffic as it snaked away towards the creeping night.

"This is my favorite time of day," I said, still gazing through the glass and overcome with a sudden sense of melancholy. "I love the color in the sky at sunset."

I turned around. Connie was sitting on the sofa with her legs crossed. She had her handbag beside her and her notebook resting in her lap.

"It's different in Europe," I said. "The sunsets seem to have different colors." I shrugged. "Maybe it's because the days are colder..."

"Do you miss Europe?"

"I miss the farm," I said. "I have enough property that I can wander around all day and not see another soul. I like that isolation. It's different here."

"How long before you fly out?"

"Two more days here, then I fly to the east coast for three days. Then back home."

"And you're in L.A. for filming, right?"

I nodded. "A couple of days of filming. But I also had some meetings with distributors earlier in the week."

Connie asked, 'Do you like L.A.?"

"Sure," I shrugged. "It's a great city – and it's the unofficial porn capital of America. It's the perfect place to work and play if you're in this industry."

Connie shook her head in surprise. "I had no idea the city had such a strong porn industry."

I stared at her. "Almost ninety percent of all porn films shot in this country are filmed down there," I pointed out into the night, "down in the San Fernando Valley."

I went to the desk and foraged in the top drawer for another cigar. I clipped the end and drew back until the tip glowed. I blew a feather of blue smoke at the ceiling and sighed. It had been a good day – two new scenes on film. When I got back to the farm I would run them through post-production. With the two scenes slated for filming tomorrow, there would be enough footage for another release. I frowned, musing over titles.

"What do you think of, *'Ricky's L.A. Adventure'*, as a title for my next DVD?" I asked suddenly.

Connie made a face like she had stepped in something on the sidewalk. "Is that the best you can come up with?" she asked. "It hardly screams, 'buy me!'."

I smiled, and nodded my head. "Good point," I admitted. I stared up at the ceiling for a moment, as if the answer might be written in big letters there. It wasn't. "How about, *'Wicked Teen Sluts of America's West Coast'*?"

"Better," she said. I went to the desk and wrote the title down on a scrap of paper.

Connie tilted her head inquisitively and narrowed her eyes. She paused for a moment, like she was searching for the right words, and then asked, "Tell me the downside. Tell me what you don't like about being a porn actor."

I didn't hesitate. I didn't have to gaze thoughtfully off into the distance because I knew the answer immediately. "Intimacy," I said. "That's the downside."

Connie leaned forward. "What do you mean?" she asked softly.

"Working in this industry comes at a cost," I said. "The price you pay is the intimacy that most people enjoy and take for granted in their lives."

"Because of all the sex?"

"Yes," I said. "It's very difficult to maintain a relationship when you work in this industry," I explained. "The sex is always physical, and it's rare that you get the opportunity to really connect with anyone on a level beyond emotionally superficial."

Connie's expression was subdued and serious. She was watching me with careful eyes.

"I miss the intimacy of a real relationship," I admitted. "I miss having that special someone in my heart and in my life. I miss kissing someone who I care deeply for, and I miss making love, Connie. I miss loving someone physically and with the emotional passion that people in love enjoy."

"That sounds sad," Connie said.

I shrugged. "This industry is demanding. It's like being a professional athlete. The best, most vibrant years of your life have to be dedicated completely to your passion if you want to succeed. Then, maybe at thirty or thirty-five, you realize your career is over because you don't have what it takes anymore to compete with the younger stars rising around you. So before the age of forty, most people in the industry are washed up and forgotten — cast aside and left to fend for themselves in a world they never really grew up in. They have no experience of love, or how to find it," I shrugged, "or what it even feels like."

Connie sat pensively for a long moment and then looked up. "You say you miss love, Rick... but to miss something so powerful means you must have experienced it..."

"Once," I said with a forlorn sigh.

"Want to tell me about it? How old were you?"

"Twenty-three," I said.

"And...?"

I sighed, overcome by a sudden sense of heaviness at the memory. "And I was living in Italy."

Connie looked intrigued. "Was the girl you fell in love with Italian?"

I nodded. "I met her when I was in Europe. I was working in porn, and had a contract with a film producer who was based in Italy, so I moved there for eight months and shot about a dozen films in that time."

"Was the girl you loved a porn actress?"

I shook my head. "No, she was a photographer. She was studying photographic art. I met her at a little sidewalk café one afternoon."

"Sounds romantic."

"She was beautiful," I said softly. "Her name was Amelia. She was living away from her family while she studied. She had a tiny little studio apartment above a pastry shop."

"What do you remember of her?"

I smiled wistfully. "Everything," I said. "She had the face of an angel, and the most beautiful smile. She smoked cheap French cigarettes and when she looked at me, I swear she could see straight through to my soul."

"I didn't know you spoke Italian."

"I didn't – and I still don't. But somehow when I was with Amelia words didn't seem important. Everything she said was in her eyes and the touch of her fingertips. It was in the way she smiled, the way she moved. She was love in motion."

I glanced up at Connie. She had her elbows propped on her knees, sitting on the edge of the sofa with her chin cupped in her hands, gazing at me.

"The first time we made love was on the rooftop of her apartment building," I smiled to myself fondly. "Amelia brought a bottle of wine and I brought a blanket, and we sat, high above the city, looking down at the lights and up at the stars. That's when I learned the difference between making love and having sex," I said. "That was the night I grew up, I suppose. Everything before that evening with Amelia was about the physical. After that night I realized I was a changed man. Something inside me had come alive... and then died again when we eventually broke up."

"How long did the romance last?"

I shook my head. "A few months," I said softly.

"Did she know you were a porn actor?"

"No. I told her I was in advertising."

Connie looked suddenly intrigued. "Why didn't you tell her what you did for a living, Rick? Were you embarrassed?"

"No," I shook my head. "I've never been embarrassed about the work I do. I'm proud of my body of work over the years. I didn't tell Amelia because I knew she wouldn't understand."

"And did the romance end when your work finished in Italy?"

"Before that," I said sadly. "One day she followed me to where we were filming," I made a helpless gesture with my hands. "She thought I was having an affair." I dropped my eyes to the floor. "In hindsight, it probably would have been better if I had been. At least that she could have understood."

"I'm sorry," Connie said in a whisper.

I looked up and smiled. "That was all a long time ago," I said like it didn't hurt anymore. "But one day... one day when I'm finished making porn films, I want that again, Connie. I want that all-consuming passion for someone. I want to love someone in the way the great poets write about it. I want to love someone so much that I know if I ever lose them my heart will break."

I needed a drink – badly.

I went into the kitchen and spent a long time staring at the litter of bottles on the counter, before mixing together a witch's brew. I drained the glass in a single gulp and prayed the numbness would come quickly while I tried to think about something else.

Connie watched me in silence. She waited until I had come back into the living room, and then glanced up at me from out of the corner of her eye. "What do you believe is the attraction of porn for men?"

"The attraction?"

She nodded. "What is it about porn films that men find so interesting?"

I smiled. "Well, I have a theory… if you would like to hear it."

"Sure." She flipped through her notebook until she found a new blank page and squirmed on the sofa for a few seconds to get herself comfortable.

"I think a lot of men watch porn films because, in their heart, they want to believe that sexy women really do exist," I said.

Connie looked nonplussed. She sprinkled me with a cold little smile. "That's it? That's your theory?"

I nodded. "That's what I believe in a nut-shell," I said. I found a half-empty bottle of rum, hidden in the litter of empty bottles on the kitchen counter. I poured myself a drink.

"A lot of men live boring lives with boring wives," I explained. "They watch porn because they want to believe that somewhere in the world, sexy nymphomaniac women really do exist. Guys want to hang on to the dream that one day a woman like the ones they watch in porn films will walk into *their* lives," I said.

Connie's head was bowed over her notebook.

"Watching porn is a way of escaping the reality of the dragon-wife they're married to who *only* wants sex once every few weeks, and then *only* in the missionary position, and *only* in the bedroom after the kids are asleep… and *only* with the lights out. And *only* for fifteen minutes." I said, then stood there, like Napoleon, with one of my hands tucked inside the opening between my shirt buttons.

(I was scratching).

Connie shook her head, but diligently wrote down everything I said.

"You don't agree with my theory?"

She looked up and shrugged. "It makes sense, I suppose," she conceded. "But if it's true, it's sad. Very sad."

I laughed. "Why?"

"Because men are using pornography as a fantasy escape. Surely there is more to life than sex. Men must realize that."

I made a wide-eyed face of mock horror. "Connie, millions of women read erotic romance novels. It's exactly the same thing. The erotica books they read are all about charming, romantic leading men. And women read them because they want to cling to the fantasy that somewhere in the world guys like that really do exist and that, maybe one day, a man like that will walk into *their* world and they can escape the overweight slob of a husband they married who *only* buys them a card on their birthdays, and *always* forgets their anniversary... and *never* takes them out to elegant restaurants." I waved my arms in the air like I was trying to throw away my hands. "Where is the difference?"

"They're harmless romance novels, for heaven's sake!" Connie gave me the sort of glare that was calculated to shrivel me into silence.

"They're mommy-porn," I countered. "They fill women's heads and imaginations with impossible fantasy men. Hell, I bet there are thousands of women around the world right now reading those books and dreaming of what it would be like to live with one of those fictional men," I gulped down the last of the rum in the bottom of my glass before going on. "Well there are just as many guys dreaming about living with one of the girls in my films. There might be slight differences in the media being used... but the message and the attractions are the same for both sexes."

Connie set aside her pen and pad. She was looking at me with a serious expression.

"Is that why you make porn films?" she asked. "To fuel those male fantasies?"

"No," I shook my head. "I make porn films to entertain. Maybe you should ask an erotic romance author why they write the books they do – whether it's to fuel women's fantasies, or merely to create an entertaining escape for readers."

"What do you think?"

I shrugged. "I don't know," I said, exasperated. "I don't write erotic romance books for women, Connie. I make porn films for men."

"Does the reality match the fantasy you create?"

I frowned. "What do you mean?"

"Are the girls in your films always the adventurous sex-hungry creatures that they portray on film?"

"No," I said, my voice flat and emphatic. "The girls in my films are generally very sexual women," I agreed, "but after filming ends, they are girlfriends and wives, daughters and mothers. They catch buses, cook dinners, do laundry. They don't spend their entire lives jumping from one bed to another. Sure, they love sex, and they love their work... but it's still work. It's not the sum of them, Connie – it's a part of them." I went to the window and stared out at the view so that I spoke my next words at the glass.

"I'm sure erotic romance authors don't write books about real people," I said. "They create leading men who might be *based* on someone they know, but the truth is that their characters are probably a mixture of reality and author fantasy. My actresses are the same."

When I finally turned back to face the room, Connie was writing notes. She finished with a sudden flourish, underlined a couple of words, then looked up to find me quietly gazing at her.

She leaned back, arched her spine to stretch, and yawned at the same time. The movement of her body thrust her breasts out and put strain on the second button of her blouse so that the top gaped open and I caught a fleeting glimpse of white lace bra and creamy soft cleavage.

I wilted theatrically, and slumped against the wall. My head dropped and I shook it from side to side as if to clear a dazed fog.

"Rick – are you okay?" I heard the sudden alarm in Connie's voice.

I glanced up. Nodded, then straightened with dramatic care. "Yes," I said bleakly. "I'll be fine in a few minutes."

The sound of concern stayed in her voice. Connie leaned forward. "What happened? What's wrong with you?"

I rubbed my forehead as though massaging away headache and tension. "I saw the lace of your bra, and I got an erection," I said, stifling a grin to draw the joke out to its punch line. "My cock... it's so big that when it gets hard it takes all the blood from my head to fill it. So I faint."

Connie's expression morphed from concern to bitter apathy. "You're joking, right?" she asked dryly.

"Maybe..."

If Connie was laughing, it was on the inside, and well concealed by an unimpressed scowl. She went on crisply.

"What is your mindset when you are performing with a woman... or several of them?"

"Do you mean my attitude?"

"No. I want to know what you are thinking about when you're performing in one of your sex scenes." Her voice changed, becoming warmer and more personal. "Are you concentrating on the girls you are working with... are you trying to get yourself off... or are you thinking about camera angles and directing the scene?"

"Aah," I suddenly understood. I was impressed. "Good question."

"Thanks," Connie brightened under even the briefest moment of flattery.

"It's difficult," I admitted. I glanced over my shoulder to the kitchen counter where I had left my glass, and regrettably decided I couldn't fetch it without enhancing Connie's belief that I had a drinking problem. I went across to the big desk and leaned against it, my arms folded across my chest. "In the back of my mind I am always thinking about the scene – where the cameras are, and what is being captured on film," I said.

"Because we don't work to a detailed script, I can't orchestrate close ups, or have a pre-production plan for what camera angles will be used at any particular moment, so the camera work is critical. My guys need to be instinctive. They need to anticipate those moments where the girl's face is going to show pleasure or ecstasy, and be ready for it.

"The actual mechanics – the physicality of a scene – could be filmed by anyone who can hold and focus a camera. It's certainly not rocket science," I smiled openly, "but the emotion and reactions of the girls – their expressions – are what makes my films so much more than just smut, so they are crucial moments that can't be replicated. The camera has to be there to capture every spontaneous instant."

"So you always have your director's cap on?" Connie lifted an eyebrow.

"Always," I confessed. "Even though my guys are the best in the business, and they know how I work, I'm always worrying that a vital expression or moan of pleasure will be missed."

"That must make performing more difficult?" Connie flushed soft color under her cheeks and she was suddenly appealing and almost child-like in the way she gazed at me.

"It can, I guess," I shrugged, "but I don't have sex on film for pleasure, Connie. I did when I first started out in this business – what guy wouldn't love every moment – but after all these years, it really is just my job."

"With benefits."

I nodded and smiled. "The benefits are obvious, but for all that, what you see of me on film is purely Rick Cassidy the porn actor, not Rick the guy."

"So you don't have sex with multiple partners in your personal life when you are away from filming?" Her smile changed slowly and the color in her cheeks darkened.

"No!" I laughed. "It's too exhausting." I pushed myself away from the desk, and glanced longingly at the kitchen counter where my glass and a fresh bottle of bourbon were waiting. When I spoke again, my voice was neutral. "I orgasm twice a day for twenty filming days each month – maximum. And these days it is becoming less because I am trying to step back from filming and bring other guys in to take my place. Like today, for example. A few years ago I would have put myself into both the scenes we shot by the swimming pool. Now, Roland and Victor are here to take one of the scenes."

"But you still enjoyed the scene with that young girl today, Rick. You certainly looked like you did."

I nodded. "Sure," I said. "I enjoy sex, Connie. And I *love* women. Part of what you saw with Lily was pleasure, and part was work. It's a good job that I enjoy," I said again, "but it's still just my job."

Connie made notes, then flicked back through the pages.

"So what is your attitude when you film?"

"You want to know how I approach a scene?"

"Yes," she said. "Do you always walk on set like a dominant Alpha male, like you did with that girl today?"

"I do," I said. "Part of that is my personality. I'm a take-charge kind of guy. Part of it is also because of my role as director. As a dominant performer I can position the girls the way I want: move them and choreograph the action to show them off in the best possible light. Without that control, some of the actresses lose their way. They're looking to be guided – they're accustomed to being compliant to the requirements of the scene."

"Is it a fine line?" Connie whispered, the words sounding husky deep in her throat.

"I guess it can be," I said, seriously considering the issue for the first time. It wasn't something I had ever thought about consciously until Connie had asked the question.

"A guy can go on set and 'fuck angry' – know what I mean?"

"I think so…"

"He can be too aggressive, be too dominating," I explained. "You can see it in his face and his gestures – and the way he is with the girl. I don't want that kind of attitude on film – not even in a gang-bang scene," I insisted. "The guys have to be firm, but there also has to be respect. I don't want my actresses being filmed as victims. They always need to be enthusiastic and willing, because with their enthusiasm they retain power. Once they are forced, or held down and taken in such a way that they are overpowered or lose their dignity because of the guy's aggression, the scene loses all of its sexiness."

Connie straightened her back and I noticed her breasts move under the silk of her blouse. "What happens when you work with a woman that doesn't turn you on? Does that happen?"

"Sometimes," I conceded. "Not very often these days, because I have the luxury of being able to pick and choose which actresses I work with, but when I was performing in other people's films there were times when the actress and I were not compatible. That makes the work difficult."

"You mean the girls you were paired with weren't pretty or sexy enough for you?"

"No – porn is full of sexy women," I said. "I'm talking about chemistry. Sometimes it's just not there."

"So what do you do? How do you keep... stay..."

"Hard?"

"Yes."

"I fuck a fantasy," I said simply. "I play out my private fantasy in my mind throughout the scene. Instead of relying on the actress to arouse me through the sexual connection, it all happens in my imagination."

Connie looked suddenly intrigued. She paused for a moment, and her expression became sly.

"Tell me your fantasy."

"No."

"Why?"

"Because it's private," I said.

She persisted. "I think a lot of readers would like to know what *really* turns Rick Cassidy on..."

I smiled, thinly. "Then tell me yours."

Connie flinched and the smile on her face twisted. "I don't have a sexual fantasy."

I stared at her, my eyebrows raised, my face full of mockery. "Really?"

"Really," she said. Her eyes flicked away. There was something unsettled in her expression that she masked quickly. "I suppose you like blondes."

"No," I countered. "I like beautiful sexy women. I don't care about the color of their hair, or the size of their breasts. I like a lady who is confident and open about her sexuality."

"Young?"

"Confident and open about their sexuality," I said again. "Fucking a teenage nymphomaniac might be every middle-aged man's fantasy, but when you've had as many teen girls as I have over the years, the attraction loses its allure. Age doesn't matter to me."

"Then why not fill your films with older women? If it's all about sexuality rather than age and appearance..." her voice rose an octave and became a challenge.

"Because on film I fuck the kind of girls that my audience wishes they could fuck," I explained calmly. "That's what sells my films. But their fantasy is not necessarily mine..."

"And your fantasy is..." Connie tried again.

"A secret," I said firmly. The smile slipped from my lips. I glanced at the big clock. It was getting late. Outside, night had fallen – the sky was black through the big glass windows.

"Then tell me where you draw the line?" Connie asked. "Where does artistic taste cross over to become something tawdry and crude?"

"That's a question that doesn't have a definitive answer," I said. "My idea of art and tasteful sex on film is something totally different to producers like John Bellamy, for instance. There are many sexual fetishes that I would never capture on film, because they don't appeal to my audience, or to my personal beliefs. They cross my line."

"So you do have a line?"

"Of course," I became incensed. "But my line clearly is very different to your line. And your line is very different to those film makers within the porn industry who feel nothing should be off limits."

"So should there be censorship?"

"Censorship by who?" I shot back. "You would censor everything beyond a chaste kiss. Some people in Washington would agree with you. Then you have the other extreme, people who insist on their right to free expression, regardless of what they wish to express." I shook my head heavily. "The audience is – and should always be – the only arbitrator of what pornography is acceptable. People vote with their money every day. They purchase the products they want, and they buy from the brands they trust. Pornography – when you boil it down to its essence – is just another product in a world-wide market. If consumers want to buy extreme porn, then it is there and available for them," I pointed a finger into the air. "But at the moment 'mainstream porn' dominates the industry."

"Mainstream porn? You mean the kind of porn that you make?"

"Yes."

Connie shifted in her chair with agitation. It had been a long day. My throat was raw from talking. Connie wiggled around again and stifled a weary yawn.

"Would you like to come to dinner with me?" I asked suddenly.

Connie blinked. "I... I can't..." she said.

I looked disbelieving. I slapped my hand over my heart, and gave her one of those sincere expressions that politicians use to get themselves elected. "I promise, it will only be dinner."

She shook her head, started stuffing her notebook into her bag. "No, really. I can't," she said again. "I have other plans."

"Can't they be postponed?"

"No." she said emphatically. "Maybe tomorrow night, if the invitation still stands," she offered to placate me.

I gave in. "Okay," I said. "Tomorrow night. It's a date."

Connie got to her feet, drew her fingers down her skirt to smooth it and pressed at her hair. She gave me a chill little smile. "It's not a date," she said. "It's a dinner. That's all."

Chapter 16.

When Connie arrived the next morning the house was unnaturally quiet. She came through the front door with a wary look of uncertain suspicion.

"Where is everybody?"

"Change of shift," I smiled. "All the girls and my two actors have gone. They left last night. Roland and Victor flew back to Europe, and the four girls have driven north to San Francisco. They have been booked for a couple of weeks of adult entertaining at one of the clubs."

Connie looked quizzical. "Adult entertaining? You want to tell me what that really means?"

"Stripping," I said. "They've got a gig pole dancing and doing some escort work for wealthy clients."

Connie didn't look shocked. Two days ago she would have been outraged.

"And your film crew? Your makeup lady?"

I jerked my head with a gesture towards the big glass doors. "They are all out by the pool relaxing," I said. "Lily is swimming laps."

Connie's expression changed to one of intrigue. "That young girl stayed here last night, Rick?"

I nodded matter-of-factly. "Bellamy is in hospital," I said, not knowing if I should be sad about that. "He asked if I could keep an eye on her for a couple of days until I fly east."

Connie folded her arms. She shifted her weight onto one leg so that her hip thrust out and her eyes became cold little things. "I bet you didn't just keep an eye on her..."

I made my eyes wide and artless. I raised an eyebrow. "You sound jealous?"

She laughed, but the sound was hollow. "I'm not," she said.

I could've told Connie that Lily slept in one of the spare rooms. I could have told her that Lily passed out drunk before midnight and I had to carry her to bed. I could have told her that nothing happened between us... but I didn't. I just smiled a slow lazy enigmatic smile and sprinkled doubt over her.

I changed the subject. "I have two local actresses due to arrive at any moment," I said. "We're filming two more scenes today to wrap up content for a new DVD."

Connie frowned just a little. "Are you doing both scenes yourself?"

I nodded. "Yes," I said. "The guys couldn't stay in town for another day, and there are no other male actors here in the States that I would trust the scene to."

Connie's face went through a range of expressions as new questions came to her and she silently resolved them.

She said nothing.

She drifted across the living room, slipped the strap of her handbag off her shoulder and left it on the sofa. She stood in the middle of the floor for a long moment and then turned around to face me – and in those brief few moments her expression had changed, like she had shrugged off her annoyance. She smiled at me brightly. "So when does filming start?"

"As soon as the two girls arrive."

"Have you worked with either of these girls before?"

"I shot two scenes with Becky going back a few years," I said. "Both those scenes were in another director's film and I haven't had the chance to work with her since. Yvette?" I paused and smiled, "Yvette is relatively new to the industry. I think she only started a year or two ago. Victor did a scene with her in another film for another producer about six months ago."

Connie was curious. "Does she come recommended?"

I smiled. "She comes loudly," I grinned.

Connie actually smiled.

"Do you want me here today? Can I stay for the filming again?" she asked.

"Of course," I said. "Tomorrow is my last day in L.A., and I know you need to get your article finished... and we have a dinner date for tonight, remember?"

The smile on her lips became something a little more natural. "How could I forget?"

I felt like there was more she was about to say. Her lips changed shape to form the words, but there was a sudden knock at the front door and whatever she was about to say was forgotten as Becky and Yvette appeared in all their spectacular Californian glory in the doorway. The two girls looked like they had come straight off the beach. They were both tanned golden brown. Becky was the tallest. She had long sun-bleached

166

hair, and the most amazing sparkling blue eyes. Her figure was athletic – she had small breasts and a lithe, slender figure. She had the longest legs I had ever seen on a woman. She was wearing a t-shirt and cut off denim shorts, her feet thrust into open sandals. She came into my arms with a friendly smile of recognition and her body melted against mine as she wrapped her arms around my neck.

"Ricky. I'm so excited about today. It's been a long time."

"Too long," I smiled warmly into her eyes. She kissed me lingeringly on the lips and then stepped back and turned to introduce Yvette. "I don't think you two have met yet."

Yvette was an inch shorter than Becky. But her figure was shaped more in the classic mold of a porn actress. Her breasts were large, her waist tiny. She had short brown hair. She stepped across the threshold and lifted herself onto tiptoes to kiss me on the cheek.

"Nice to meet you, Mr. Cassidy," her smile was genuine and friendly.

"Nice to meet you, Yvette," my eyes roamed over her body, lingering on her breasts for a second or two. "And call me Rick."

Yvette held up a handbag. "I brought this with me," she said.

"A costume change?" I asked curiously.

She was wearing hip-hugging denim jeans and a thin strip of fabric, the width of a bandage that did little more than cover the hard jut of her nipples.

"Honey, you won't need a costume change," I smiled wolfishly. "This is a porn film. Everyone is going to want to see your beautiful body naked."

Yvette's eyes grew wide and she giggled. "I didn't bring any costumes. These are just vibrators and dildos," she explained. "You told Becky on the phone that you wanted a lot of lesbian action, yeah?"

I nodded and then smiled. "I like a girl who comes prepared."

"I hope you like a girl who comes loudly," she laughed.

"That," I said with a sly grin, "is a very definite bonus."

I introduced the actresses to Connie and then the girls arranged themselves attentively on the sofa.

I stood before them and they looked up at me as though expecting some grand speech. I didn't have one. All I had was the idea for the scene we were about to shoot that morning. So I laid it out for them.

"We're going to shoot the first scene in the main bedroom," I said, massaging my temple between thumb and fingertips, visualizing the scene as I explained it. "We're going to do one shot filmed from inside the bedroom that will show you two girls outside the window. I want you to be peaking through the glass, and you'll be looking at me. I will be laying on the bed naked and pretending to be asleep. You girls will point and make some sexy faces and then disappear out of shot as if you are going to come inside. Make sense?"

Becky and Yvette nodded.

"Then we will shoot the rest of the action in one long take in the bedroom. There will be a couple of cameras, and I have moved the furniture to position a long red leather sofa under the window. I want you girls to come into the bedroom, spend a few moments silently admiring me," I explained, "and then I will wake up."

"And then what?" Becky asked.

"I want you two girls to make out on the sofa," I said. "Pretend you are putting on a sexy show for me. I will come awake, see you girls kissing and fingering each other, and I'll slowly start to stroke my cock." I pointed a finger at the girls to stress the next point. "Play out the lesbian shots," I said. "Take your time. Enjoy each other's bodies. When it appears as though I can't possibly take any more of this sexy, erotic teasing, I will come over to the sofa and then we'll just shoot a standard threesome."

I stood there, wondering if there was anything else I needed to say. Yvette and Becky were nodding their understanding, and I trusted them both enough to know what to do when the cameras started rolling.

I turned suddenly to Connie. "Would you like to be involved in this scene?"

Connie went white. I think she swallowed her tongue. She did a kind of epileptic flapping with her arms like she was trying to take flight. "No! Are you crazy?" There was a high note of alarm in her voice – a voice that I thought would seldom sound alarmed. She wrapped her arms around her shoulders in a way that made me feel like I was solely responsible for a sudden drop in room temperature.

I shook my head and held up my hands to placate her like I was expecting her to lunge at me. "Take it easy," I appeased. "I don't expect you to perform, Connie. I don't want you to join in the sex scene... but I have a spare camera, and I was wondering whether – since you're going to be watching the scene anyhow – if you would mind filming through a crack in the closet door."

Connie's arms fell to her side without her ever levitating off the sofa. She slumped back, the air sucked from her lungs. "You want me to film?" she asked slowly.

"If you wouldn't mind," I said. "I just had this idea of some secret voyeur footage that I could edit into the finished film. If Walter gets a shot of the closet door being open, and a viewer gets a sense that a mysterious person is watching the sex scene play out, it might add a new dimension to the scene. Then, if I add any footage you shoot, it all becomes more real."

Connie turned her head from side to side like she was looking for the nearest exit. "What about your makeup lady? What about Lily? Surely she could do it?"

I shook my head. "Jilian will need to be on standby in case we cut and the girls need their makeup touched," I said. "And Lily has only just started in the industry. She's an actress... and besides, I couldn't trust her to stay in the closet once the sex starts. The kid is just as likely to throw herself into the scene."

"I don't know anything about cameras or filming," Connie flustered, flailing about for excuses like she was drowning.

"It's easy," I waved away her protest with a flick of my hand. "All you have to do is point and hold the camera steady. Walter will have everything set up for you – nothing more to do."

Becky and Yvette turned their faces to Connie. Their expressions were eager and bubbling with enthusiasm. "That would be so cool," Becky enthused.

Connie held out for a few more seconds, but the pressure proved overwhelming. She surrendered with a sigh. "Okay," she said softly and then her voice rose again as she stared directly into my eyes. "But I make no promises. I can't guarantee you'll be able to use a single second of what I film."

My triumphant smile spread slowly and warmly across my lips like a tropical sunrise. "Understood," I said.

I led the actresses outside into the bright morning sunlight and introduced them to my cameramen. Jilian clucked and cooed about with her paints and powders while I took Connie into the bedroom and sat her down on the edge of the bed.

"Thanks," I said with sincerity. "I know I put you in a spot out there. I appreciate your help."

Connie's lips were thin and pale. "Just remember that I make no promises," she warned without any anger in her voice and waggled one of her fingers at me. "Don't blame me if this turns into a fiasco."

I shook my head. "It won't," I assured her. "You can't do any damage to the camera, and even if you film sixty minutes of footage with your thumb over the lens, it won't be an issue. All I'm looking for is a little bonus footage. My guys will capture everything essential."

I went to the closet and pulled the doors wide open. "There's plenty of space for you to stand," I said with the sort of encouraging voice and cheerful smile that a real estate agent uses when showing a home to a prospective purchaser. "And you don't have to do anything special. We are not filming a new Indiana Jones movie. All you have to do is try to hold the camera steady and keep it on the girls."

"Really? Just the girls?" Connie questioned. What about you?"

"You will be filming across the bed," I explained. "If the camera is on the girls then I will automatically be in the foreground of all your shots, and once the threesome starts, I will be where the girls are."

Connie nodded. She rose from the bed and came and stood beside me. She stared into the empty space of the full-length closet for a hesitant moment as though she expected something dark and dangerous to leap out at her, and then stepped inside. She pulled the doors closed behind her, leaving an inch of open gap. "This much?"

"Maybe another inch or two," I considered. "I'll check with Walter about that. I don't want the shot to have the door in it."

It took another thirty minutes before everyone was in place and we were ready to start filming.

172

Jilian took the girls outside and held them to one side of the window while I got undressed and stretched out naked on the bed. My cock hung heavy against my thigh. Walter got into position and the cameras started rolling.

"Action!" I shouted and then closed my eyes and let everyone do their job.

I heard tapping against the glass and the muted sounds of the girl's giggling. I kept my breathing deep and sonorous and counted to one hundred in my mind, and then sat up. "Well?" I turned my head to Walter.

The cameraman nodded. "Done," he said. He dropped onto the edge of the bed and played back the footage of the two girls as they seemed to discover me through the uncurtained window.

The film ran for no more than thirty seconds, but it was good.

I nodded. "Okay, bring the girls inside and we'll start with you shooting them coming through the door and then setting up for their sex show."

The simple task took twenty minutes. Connie handled the camera like a veteran. She positioned herself in the closet and Walter did a quick check on the angles with her.

He turned to me. "We're ready," he announced.

I laid back down on the bed. Walter drifted around the room and then when everything was set he made the call for 'action'.

A few seconds later I heard the bedroom door creak open and the trilling sound of Becky's giggle.

Through the narrowed slits of my eyes I watched as the scene unfolded and the girls came to stand before the foot of the bed.

Yvette was holding an eight-inch long vibrator in her hand. She sucked it into her mouth to moisten it and then the girls embraced and Becky pulled down Yvette's top and sucked her breast into her mouth. The girls writhed together, standing at the foot of the bed. Yvette's hand slithered down Becky's body and reached inside the denim of her short shorts. All the while, they were looking in my direction, watching me as I feigned sleep on the bed.

The two girls whispered softly to each other and then I saw Yvette nod her head enthusiastically. They peeled off their clothes, taking turns to undress each other until they were standing in just their heels. Becky took Yvette by the hand and led her across to the big red sofa below the window. Yvette got onto her hands and knees and I saw Walter take the camera in close for a shot of the young girls smooth, shaved sex before Becky knelt on the floor and slowly swiped her tongue along the length of the other actress's slit. I heard Yvette shudder and moan softly. Becky swatted her playfully on the butt cheek and then pulled the girl's firm cheeks apart to give her tongue better access.

The camera panned back to show both girls. Yvette was squirming. Her eyes were closed, her mouth open. Yvette's hands were digging into the leather upholstery, squeezing as Becky's tongue created delicious sensations between her parted thighs.

The vibrator lay momentarily forgotten on the sofa, Becky snatched it up with a wicked grin and sucked it into her mouth with slow deliberation. Yvette's eyes came open. She saw the vibrator between Becky's lips, and Walter moved the camera to get a wide-eyed shot of Yvette looking excited and giggling breathlessly.

"This is for you," Becky whispered. She licked her tongue across the end of the vibrator and then pressed the bulbous tip of it against the open lips of young Yvette's pussy. Yvette laid her head on the cool leather of the sofa and reached back with both of her hands to pull herself open. She was smiling – a sexy smile of anticipation and I chose that moment as the instant that I came awake on the bed. Walter was filming the girls, but I knew Connie's camera would capture me rising up onto my elbow as I stared at the girls with a look of bewildered disbelief.

The girls hadn't noticed me.

Becky sucked the vibrator into her mouth one last time and then eased it into Yvette's open pussy.

Yvette's mouth fell open and then she trapped her lip between her teeth and writhed her body as the vibrator disappeared inside her. She lifted herself up onto one elbow to change the angle. Her back was arched and she gave a long sexy sigh as the vibrator filled her.

"You like that?" Becky asked.

Yvette nodded her head and then closed her eyes again as if to concentrate on the sensations of the vibrator slowly sliding in and out of her pussy. I watched them from the bed, genuinely enchanted by the expressions on young Yvette's face. The girl wasn't acting.

Becky turned her head suddenly and saw me lying on the bed watching the performance. She smiled and gave Yvette another playful slap on her bottom. "He is watching us," Becky said softly. "He is awake."

Walter drew back and the camera swung to me on the bed and then moved again so that I was included in the action.

I sat upright, and my erection began to thicken and harden.

On the sofa, Becky slowly withdrew the vibrator from Yvette's pussy and reached around to present it to the younger girl's open mouth.

"Suck it," Becky insisted.

Yvette took the rubber cock into her mouth hungrily and sucked her own juices across her tongue and then handed the toy back to Becky.

"More?"

Yvette nodded. "Please," she sighed.

Becky slid the vibrator all the way inside Yvette's pussy and held it there for long moments while the young girl, spread on the sofa before her, began to rock her hips as though enjoying a slow gentle fuck.

I stood up and went across to where the girls played on the sofa. My cock was now hard. I stroked myself slowly as I watched the girls close up.

Becky took the vibrator from Yvette's pussy and crawled around the edge of the sofa until the two girls were kissing. She had the rubber cock held up between their lips and the two girls took turns engulfing it into their mouths.

Yvette looked up into my eyes. "We want your cock," her voice husked.

"Fuck her first," I insisted, nodding my head at Becky. "I want to watch you use the vibrator on her tight pussy before I give you my cock."

The girls changed positions. Becky got onto her hands and knees and Yvette crawled off the sofa and knelt behind her. Becky's long blonde hair hung down like a shimmering curtain and her firm pointed breasts moved with her arms as she arched her back and braced herself with her knees parted. Yvette slid the tip of the vibrator along the pouting lips of Becky's sex.

Yvette looked to me. "Do you want me to lick her first?"

I nodded.

Yvette lunged forward and slid her tongue between the folds of Becky's sex.

"Oh, I love that," Becky groaned. "Put your tongue inside."

Yvette devoured Becky's pussy with her tongue and lips, eating her sex with ravenous passion and enthusiasm. Becky threw back her head and screwed her eyes shut, squirming her hips and riding the young actresses tongue with obvious pleasure.

"Now, fuck her," I urged.

Yvette nodded and smiled. She pressed the vibrator with slow steady pressure into Becky's pussy.

Midmorning light filtered through the windows, bathing the girls in warm golden color. Sparkling shards of sunlight glinted off the rings and bracelets the girls wore.

"Oh, fuck yes," Becky moaned as the vibrator disappeared deep inside her. She rocked herself back, swinging her body from her knees in a slow sensual grind. Her mouth fell open in a sigh of satisfaction and she looked back over her shoulder to urge Yvette on. "Deeper," she insisted.

Yvette withdrew the vibrator and licked the length of it, then sucked it into her mouth. She pushed the toy back deep inside Becky's pussy. The girl on her knees shuddered and clenched her teeth together in a moment of exquisite delight.

"Yesssss," she hissed through her teeth.

I took a step closer. The two girls looked up at me.

"You want to fuck us?" Yvette asked.

Becky joined in. "Give us your cock," she begged throatily. "Please let us fuck you."

Yvette turned her body to show me the gap of her sex between her thighs. Becky reached between her legs and rubbed the flat of her palm against her clit. Her whole body began to undulate, writhing from her hips. Yvette rose slowly to her feet and came to me, swaying her hips provocatively. She threw her arms around me and kissed me. Becky watched on from the sofa, her hand moving in quickening circles over her sex. I pushed Yvette back onto her knees before me. She went willingly. She took my cock in her hand and stroked it, looking up into my eyes for an instant and then thrusting me down her throat. Her mouth worked quickly, sucking on the first few inches of my shaft while her hand stroked me at the same time.

Becky came up onto her knees, thighs spread wide on the sofa. She had two fingers pressed inside of herself, watching as I fucked Yvette's mouth. I put my hand on the back of Yvette's head and clenched a handful of her short brown hair. I pulled her mouth forward and slid more of myself between her lips. She splayed her fingers wide on my thighs to hold herself steady and rocked her body in time with each thrust.

Walter brought the camera in tight on Yvette's face as my shaft slid back and forth. The girl's eyes were closed, her brow furrowed in concentration. I used her mouth until my cock was rock hard and glistening wet. Becky slinked off the sofa and dropped to her knees beside Yvette.

"My turn," she said. Yvette took my cock from her mouth and Becky engulfed me. As she sucked her hand stayed pressed against her sex. Yvette looked on with fascination and rising arousal. I saw her touch herself as Becky gasped for breath and continued to suck me.

My cock went from one girl's mouth to the other for several minutes while Walter brought the camera in close and then drifted away for wide shots. After a few minutes, I dropped onto the sofa, thighs wide apart, my cock stiff and vaulting. The girls crouched on the cold leather on either side of me and both leaned across my body. Becky wrapped her fingers around the base of my shaft and pulled me back into her mouth. Yvette nuzzled her lips between my thighs and then moved her open mouth up and down the length of me. The girls were ravenous. I reached between Becky's spread legs and slid a finger inside her pussy and then slid sideways on the sofa and pulled her down on top of me. Her legs fell open astride my shoulders and I craned my neck forward to lick at the lips of her sex.

Becky pulled her mouth off my cock and groaned as my tongue hit the sensitive nub of her clit. I saw Walter swoop in for another close up shot and I caught a glimpse of Yvette taking me deep down her throat. I bucked my hips, thrusting myself between her lips.

I concentrated on licking Becky's clit and left the girls to take turns working my cock over with their mouths. I could feel their hot breath, the touch of their fingers, the press of their lips. I drove my tongue deep between the lips of Becky's pussy and she wiggled, then ground her sex hard against me.

I heard the two girls moan as they feasted on the length of my shaft. I saw flickers of movement around me from my two cameramen as they worked the scene from different angles. I slapped Becky on the cheek of her butt and she squealed with delight.

"Suck him, sweetie," I heard Becky say, and then an instant later I felt my cock disappear more deeply into Yvette's mouth. I slid from beneath Becky's spread legs and rolled her over onto her hands and knees on the sofa. I signaled Yvette over with a wave of my hand.

"Spread her cheeks for me," I told the young girl. She kissed me and then knelt beside Becky with her hands splayed on the tanned brown flesh of her bottom.

I got to my feet. My cock was as hard as an iron bar. Becky turned her head and glanced over her shoulder at me with a smoldering look of desire in her eyes. Yvette placed the tip of my cock against the hot lips of Becky's sex and then watched with hungry eyes as I eased myself inside of the blonde.

Yvette sat back on the sofa and spread her legs wide. I moved Becky and then placed my hand in the small of her back, pushing her down until her mouth was over Yvette's sex. Becky's tongue flicked out and licked across Yvette's clit as I began to thrust inside her. Yvette's eyes rolled up into the back of her head and her mouth fell open. She put her hand on the back of Becky's head and held her pretty face between her parted legs. The cameras moved in close for tight shots of Becky licking pussy and then came back and shot from over my shoulder, capturing the drive of my hips and the look of ecstasy on Yvette's face.

Becky turned her cheek and moaned. "Oh, fuck. Your cock is so big."

I kept thrusting, our connected bodies swaying and rocking, and then pulled my cock from Becky's pussy and stood on the sofa, straddling Yvette. Her mouth was open and I thrust myself between her lips. I drove my cock in and out of her mouth and Yvette leaned her head back passively to take me down her throat.

"Me," Becky said. "Fuck me again."

I shuffled back and put one foot on the armrest for balance and then drove myself back inside the tight warmth between Becky's flared lips. She moaned, and then sucked in a deep breath of satisfaction.

When I felt Becky's pussy begin to tighten and grip in a series of rippling spasms, I eased myself from within her and reached for Yvette's hand.

"I want you on your knees," I insisted.

Yvette went willingly, folding herself on the sofa, positioning her body in willing invitation for me. Becky crept between the girl's parted thighs and spent long minutes with her tongue between Yvette's legs before I slapped her on the butt and ordered her aside.

Yvette looked over her shoulder and parted her legs a little wider. Becky took my cock in her hand and guided me into Yvette's pussy.

The young girl squealed as I disappeared inside her. She splayed her fingers wide on the red leather and began to whimper and gasp with every thrust. Becky crawled around us and stifled Yvette's sighs with a long lingering sexy kiss.

My cock became quickly coated in the juices of Yvette's sex. I slid myself from her pussy and offered myself to Becky's mouth. She licked the tip of my shaft almost tentatively and then smiled with mischief. She took me into her mouth until Yvette's juices were thick on her lips.

"Fuck her again," Becky insisted.

I guided my cock back into Yvette's pussy and began to move my body with more determination. Each thrust slammed our bodies together and I felt Yvette began to tremble beneath me.

"My god. I think I'm going to come," Yvette rasped softly. She reached back between her thighs with one hand and her fingers moved furiously over her clit as I continued to thrust inside her.

She cried out suddenly and then the sound dissolved into a series of high pitched indecipherable squeals. Her body went rigid for a long moment and then she lowered her head to the sofa, every muscle turned to jelly.

Becky kissed the girl passionately, and for long moments I was forgotten as the two actresses embraced and their tongues entwined in a slow sexy dance. I eased my cock from Yvette's spent pussy and stroked myself slowly, watching these two gorgeous young women making out. Yvette was soft and limp in Becky's arms as the blonde's hands gently kissed the young girl's breast and throat and neck. Yvette's eyes were closed, her face dreamy and distant. When the two girls broke apart, Yvette curled up in a corner of the sofa and lay gently stroking her pussy and watching on.

I rolled Becky onto her back and she spread her legs wide. She was undulating her hips as she gently fingered herself. I stepped forward and my cock went all the way inside her pussy in the first fluent stroke. Becky threw back her head and clenched her jaw. I felt her hands reach for my hips to hold me inside her. I lowered myself onto one knee for better balance and began to build up a steady fucking rhythm. Becky began to thrill. Her grunts and groans became more desperate – more frantic. Yvette crawled languidly across to where the blonde lay and began to cover her body with kisses, starting at her throat and then sucking her breasts, kissing her way down to where my cock drove deep inside.

I felt myself tense and tighten. I felt each thrust become more urgent with my own rising need. Yvette seemed to sense it too. She had her cheek resting on the flat of Becky's stomach, watching my cock disappear inside the blonde's smooth sex. She turned her eyes up to read my expression and then licked her lips lasciviously.

That was it.

That was all it took.

I withdrew myself and the instant my cock was free, Yvette craned her neck forward to take me in her mouth. I threw my head back as I felt the last shreds of my control tear away. Walter scurried quickly for a close up as I erupted over Yvette's mouth and cheeks.

The scene ended with the two girls kissing between the spent and slowly softening length of my shaft. When I saw the two cameramen begin to glide away for wide shots, I called cut and then dropped onto the sofa as my legs failed and went from beneath me in exhaustion.

Chapter 17.

We gathered casually around the swimming pool for lunch. The caterers had arrived with more trays of tasteless sandwiches that looked like they were made from cardboard. Everyone was in a good mood – the morning scene had gone off without a hitch, and I sat under the shade of an umbrella and played back the footage that Connie had filmed from within the closet.

It was good. Surprisingly good.

Connie had managed to capture every moment of the sex scene, and even the occasional tilt of the lens only served to give a stronger voyeuristic impression as I watched the scene in playback. For several minutes, at different stages, I could see the shadowy figures of my cameramen as they crossed into shot, but after editing those out I realized I had a great deal of useable film.

Connie sat on a chair opposite me, watching my face intently.

I looked up and smiled. "You did a terrific job," I said, meaning it. "I really am impressed. This is going to add a wonderful extra dimension to the scene."

Connie was taken completely off balance by the compliment and my sincerity. All the tension and haughtiness spilled from her and suddenly she became like a little girl, with a blush of pleased and shy color washing over her cheeks.

"I'm glad," she said softly. "It's not the kind of job I would ever like to do for a living."

"Really?"

Connie nodded. "Too much pressure," she said. "I was conscious every moment that I couldn't afford to shake or move or even blink for fear of missing some scene that might be important to you."

"It's a long way from journalism, I suppose," my lips wrapped around a gentle grin.

Connie nodded. "With journalism, I get to write and then rewrite, and then send it off to an editor who polishes my words and makes me look better than I really am. Nothing spontaneous happens in journalism. Everything I produce has the benefit of deliberation."

Lily went skipping passed on the hot pavers, splashing and dripping water. She reached the edge of the pool and dived in, her entry into the water far from elegant. The pool erupted and then she emerged in a froth of bubbles, gasping and giggling.

"Come on in," Lily cried, waving frantically at me to get my attention. "The water is beautiful."

I didn't believe her. As she bounced around in the pool, her nipples looked so hard they might snap off and her arms and shoulders were covered in a rash of goose bumps.

I had been in that pool just yesterday. I knew damn well the water wasn't beautiful. It wasn't warm. It wasn't even cool. It was fucking freezing.

I waved back to Lily. "I'm busy," I said.

Lily would not be deterred. "What about you, journalist lady?"

Connie's expression turned to stone. "I don't have a swimsuit," she said flatly.

The young girl shrugged her shoulders. "So what? I'm nude."

Connie looked wearily at me. "Really?" she raised an eyebrow.

I shrugged. "It's the idiotic enthusiasm of youth," I lamented like an old man. "Ignore her."

Lily splashed about for a few more seconds and then swum off towards the far end of the pool to annoy the cameramen. I turned back to Connie.

"Do you have any questions that you want to ask me for your article while we're on a break?"

Connie looked like I had surprised her. "Um... how long is the break before you start filming again?"

I looked up at the sun. "We probably have about an hour," I estimated. "I want to shoot the next scene outdoors."

Connie leaned forward. "Another pool scene?"

I shook my head. "There is a garden just over there," I gestured with my head beyond the high fence that surrounded the pool area. "It's isolated from view. The whole area has been landscaped. I thought it would make a great location."

"And you're waiting for what?" she asked.

"The sun," I said. "I have this thing about shadows when I shoot outdoor scenes. The last thing I want is the shadows of my camera guys falling over the actresses as they perform." I shrugged. "When the sun is a little lower we will start filming."

Connie didn't say anything, but I got the sense that some secret little part of her was mildly impressed. Maybe she was starting to believe that, to me, my films were more than just graphic sex.

Connie stared off into the distance for a long moment like she was looking for something. "Have you ever thought about retiring from the industry, Rick?"

"At least once a week," I smiled — but I wasn't really joking. "I am not enjoying the performing side of my work anymore," I admitted. "Not like I used to."

"Is that because you're thirty? Is that old for a male actor in porn?"

I shook my head. "There are lots of male actors who are just hitting their stride at my age," I said. "The porn industry is a lot more forgiving with male actors than it is with the girls. Because a guy's physical appearance is secondary to a scene, no one really cares too much about how he looks. As I've said before — it's all about the girls. Most of them get out of the industry before they turn thirty. They do their films, they make some money, and they get out before they burn out."

"So if it's not your age, then why aren't you enjoying it anymore?"

I shrugged my shoulders heavily. "I think I'm just jaded," I said. "I've made hundreds of films, and slept with maybe a thousand women. Maybe more. The truth is that everything about performing that was so special and such a turn-on has lost its luster."

Connie watched me carefully. "Would you stay in the porn industry if you retired from performing?"

"Sure," I said. "I love the directing, and I like working with the actors and actresses. They are all good people. And I like producing films and all the behind the scenes logistics that goes into creating DVDs and downloads." I stabbed a finger into the air. "And don't forget," I said lastly, "I have a considerable investment in technology and property back in France. Money I have sunk into the farm is for the future."

"Do you think you really could give up performing? How would you go, suddenly not having sex so many times with so many women?"

"I honestly don't know," I confessed. "Maybe after a couple of years I would get bored and come out of retirement, like a pro footballer who doesn't know the right time to walk away. Maybe I would have trouble adjusting to a monogamous kind of lifestyle. I guess I won't know for sure until the day I decide."

We left it there. Connie disappeared inside the house, and I figured she was going to make notes. I gathered the cast and crew around me and they followed me single file beyond the pool area and into the gardens.

"We're going to shoot here," I announced. "I want everyone ready in thirty minutes. Lily," I singled the young girl out. "Do you want to do this scene with me?"

Lily nodded her head and I thought it might fall off her shoulders. "Rick, that would be fab!" she gushed.

"Fine," I said. "We'll do the scene with you and Becky together. Yvette," I turned to the sexy young girl standing beside me, "you can take the afternoon off."

Yvette looked a little disappointed, but that might have been my imagination.

(or my ego).

I spent fifteen minutes laying out the scene for my cameramen, and Walter and I talked about alternative angles and how we would handle the changing light as it began to filter through the high trees overhead.

When I got back to the house, Jilian was doing makeup and Connie was staring out through the big windows, down into the valley below.

"Penny for your thoughts."

Connie turned slowly, her mind still somewhere beyond the window. "I was thinking about dinner tonight," she lied so smoothly that I almost believed her. "I was wondering what restaurant you were going to take me to, and whether I had time to get my hair done?"

I played along. "We're going to a cozy little restaurant called 'Still Water'," I said. "Very elegant, very swish. And your hair looks fabulous."

Chapter 18.

The scene opened with Becky and Lily holding hands. The two girls were wearing short summer dresses. There was a small rustic bridge in the garden built over a landscaped stream that meandered through the property. The girls came towards the camera, reached the bridge and paused there for a long lingering kiss. Becky wrapped her arms around Lily's waist and gripped the rail of the bridge behind her so that the two girls were pressed tight together. Lily's hand drifted down onto Becky's bottom and the two girls smiled sexily at each other. Becky's hands began to roam over Lily's fresh young body, raising the hem of her dress so that the camera caught a glimpse of the younger blonde's lace panties high on her hips. Lily's hands were caressing Becky's body. She tangled her fingers into Becky's hair and pulled her face close so that their tongues danced against each other. Becky deftly unbuttoned the top of Lily's dress and cupped one of the young girl's firm tanned breasts in the palm of her hand.

I stood off camera, watching. The chemistry between the two girls was incredibly erotic. They looked fresh and sexy, and I prayed that Walter and my second cameraman were capturing close ups and wide shots.

There was a gentle breeze in the background, swaying through the trees and palms. It ruffled Lily's hair and fluttered against the fabric of the girl's dresses, swishing their skirts. I couldn't take my eyes off Becky. She was taller than Lily – a

191

statuesque blonde – with an incredible sexuality that just seemed to ooze from every pore of her perfect body. I watched, transfixed, knowing that Becky would steer the action comfortably until I made my entrance.

Lily pulled Becky's dress open, which was my cue to enter the scene. I paused for just a moment. Becky had her head thrown back, her face tilted into the warm afternoon sun as Lily's hands slid down and cupped Becky's breasts. Becky hummed a delicious sound of delight in the back of her throat.

I stepped out of the foliage and began to walk towards where the girls stood on the bridge.

For a long moment, neither girl noticed me. They were completely enchanted with each other's bodies. Becky pushed one thigh between Lily's legs and kissed the girl with ravenous hunger.

I had reached the bridge. I stood watching the two actresses until they broke their kiss, suddenly realizing they were being watched. They broke apart and turned to me. Lily's hand brushed across my cock that was already stiff inside my jeans. Becky cupped my face in the palms of her hand and pulled my head down to hers for a long erotic kiss. In the corner of my eye, I saw my second cameraman move from his position and step into the ankle-deep water of the stream to get a side-shot of the action while Walter hovered, coming in closer in a series of measured steps.

I turned my attention back to the two girls. Becky ran her hands across my chest and then reached to pull my t-shirt off. I put my hands above my head. The t-shirt came off and I stood bare-chested on the bridge. Lily smiled at me sweetly. She ran her hands over my body, and as I looked into her eyes, I saw Becky drop to her knees before me. She ran the palm of her hand against the swell of my cock and then unfastened the button of my jeans. My erection sprang free and Lily dropped to her knees beside Becky so that the two girls could take me in their mouths.

I gripped the rail of the bridge with one hand. Becky took the base of my shaft in her hand and held my cock before Lily's willing lips. Lily sucked me into her mouth, and then fluttered her tongue along the length of my shaft. Becky joined in. The two girls were squatting side by side on the bridge, cupping each other's breasts and kissing the length of my shaft between their wet lips.

"I want him," Lily said softly. She pulled my cock away from Becky and engulfed me with a sudden effort of concentration. Walter came close to capture the length of me disappearing down the young actress's throat. I braced my legs and gripped the far rail with my free hand. I thrust my hips forward as Lily's hot mouth swirled and sucked the swollen end of me. I remembered what John Bellamy had said at the restaurant – and he was right – this young girl had an amazing mouth. What made her so good at sucking cock was her raw enthusiasm. She had the ability to soften and then intensify the press of her lips, coupled with an obvious passion and desire to please. I stared down into her smiling face, and then Becky playfully nudged her aside.

"It's my turn," Becky said. The girls smiled into each other's faces and then Becky took over. She wrapped her lips around me while Lily watched on with close fascination.

Becky's mouth was like a warm wet tunnel for my cock. She took me deeply between her lips and then wrapped her fingers lightly around my shaft and began to work her hand and mouth together in a slow seductive rhythm. I felt my hips begin to rock and pulse, matching the beat of her mouth and the stroke of her fingers. When Lily took over again, she sucked me with sudden enthusiasm. Her eyes were closed in complete concentration, her mouth just taking the swollen crown of me so that her movements were rapid and energetic. Becky swayed back on her haunches and lowered her mouth to Lily's breast as it gently rocked to the lunges of her bobbing head.

I could hear the bubbling sound of the stream passing underneath the bridge. The garden was full of bird song. Lily rose to her feet and slid her dress off her shoulders. She was wearing black satin panties cut high up on her hips. She hooked her thumbs inside the elastic waistband and slid them off. Becky stayed on her knees and took me back inside her mouth as I wrapped a hand around Lily's waist and pulled her close to me. I turned Lily so that we were standing almost side by side. I slid my hand over her bottom. She shuffled her feet apart and wrapped one arm around my shoulder, as my finger slipped along the moist folds of her sex. Becky turned her head and gave Lily's clit a playful lick. Lily gave a sudden gasp. Becky buried her tongue between the young girl's folds and then moved her mouth to engulf me once more. I sucked one of Lily's breasts into my mouth and the young girl fisted her fingers in the hair at the back of my neck and closed her eyes in a sudden groan of pleasure.

"Lick her pussy again," I said.

Becky lifted her eyes to mine and she was smiling around my cock. She turned her head and Lily shuffled her feet wider apart. My finger slipped inside her from behind and Becky's tongue began to ravage her clit. Finally Becky slowly rose to her feet. She turned her back to me, slid the dress off her shoulders and then pulled her panties slowly down. She bent at the waist to kick them off and as she did, my fingers reached for her pussy. She was wet. She groaned, and her mouth fell open. She moved just a little so that my cock was pressed against her sex. She raised herself onto tiptoes then gripped one hand on the railing of the bridge and with the other she reached back behind her to guide my cock inside her while Lily looked on with an expression of rapt fascination. The look on Becky's face was one of pure and deep satisfaction as several inches of my shaft disappeared into her from behind. She was standing upright, her back arched so that she could look over her shoulder and see me disappearing inside her. Her mouth was wide open and her whole body shuddered.

I began to fuck her with slow gentle thrusts. My back was braced against one rail of the bridge. Becky gripped the opposite rail and began to use the leverage to rock herself back and forth on my cock. I cupped Lily's breasts in my hands and fingered her pussy.

Becky's body was exquisite – a gift of the Gods. She had the most amazing figure and the fit of our bodies together felt perfect. I began to increase the tempo of my thrusts. Becky tightened her grip on the rickety rail and threw her head back into the bright afternoon sunshine. When I slid myself from within her pussy, Lily dropped quickly to her knees. She crouched between our bodies and began to suck me, licking and tasting the juice of Becky's sex. Becky bent over the rail and my fingers once again went to work on the wetness of her sex. She began to groan, her body undulating against the push of my fingers until Lily took me from her mouth and guided me back deep inside Becky's pussy. We fucked in a rocking rhythm for several minutes and my attention was constantly drawn to the expressions of lust and delight that played across the gorgeous blonde's face.

If she was acting, she was good.

If she wasn't acting, *I* was good.

The demands of the scene meant that this couldn't go on forever. I eased myself from within Becky and turned my attention to Lily. The young actress folded herself over the railing and presented her parted legs to me. I slid myself deeply inside her in a single thrust and she licked her lips and then moaned with a sound of contentment. The bridge began to rock. Becky came to me and we kissed while I fucked the younger blonde. Lily's mouth was open in the shape of a perfect 'O'. She had her elbows resting on the rail, glancing back over her shoulder as Becky and I kissed passionately.

"Harder!" Lily grunted. "Fuck me harder."

I began to drive my hips in long pumping thrusts. Lily pushed back from the railing to grind her pussy against me and take every inch of my shaft between her legs. Becky turned and leaned over the rail beside Lily. She looked over her shoulder at me, and whispered, "Do you want me now?"

I slid my cock from Lily's pussy and plunged it back inside Becky. Lily reached back between her legs and began to rub and finger her clit, then she dropped to her knees beside me. She took my cock from Becky's pussy for a moment and sucked me into her mouth.

"I want to taste your come," Lily groaned. "Fuck her until you're ready to explode, and then give it to me."

She placed the swollen head of my shaft against Becky's pussy and once again we moved quickly into a grinding dancing rhythm between our bodies. I could feel myself beginning to thrill. I could feel the tightness in my groin clenching like a fist and I knew that my orgasm was fast approaching. Becky — an experienced actress — sensed it too. She let my cock slip from inside her and she turned around quickly and dropped to her knees beside Lily.

I was on the brink of coming. The girls devoured me with their mouths until I could hold back no longer.

"I'm going to come!" I cried out. I threw my head back. The heat of the afternoon sun washed over my face — and an instant later, I erupted.

For a long moment, I saw nothing but stars. My senses were reeling, my vision exploding into bright pinwheels of light behind my eyes. I felt the knot in the pit of my guts unravel, and when I looked down and my eyes cleared, I saw Lily's face splashed and dripped with my seed and Becky's tongue lapping at the younger girl's face.

Walter swooped in for the final close up of the girls together as my second cameraman came trudging from out of the stream. He looked satisfied. He gave me a wink and a nod and I knew the scene would be a good one. The chemistry between the girls, the idyllic garden setting and the sheer beauty of the two women I had filmed with would guarantee a special scene.

I slumped with my back against the rail of the bridge until Walter glanced at me and gave me a 'thumbs up' sign. "We're done," he smiled.

I was still breathing raggedly. The thrill for a man standing when he orgasms is always more intense than if he's laying or sitting down at the moment he comes. My legs were still trembling.

"Great work, girls," I grinned and then glanced over my shoulder to where Connie had been standing quietly off set while we filmed. She was writing notes, but somehow instinctively seemed to sense my eyes on her. She glanced up from the notepad and gazed at me with an expression that was completely unreal.

Chapter 19.

Lily and Becky showered together while I sat with my two cameramen, playing back the footage of the scene we had just shot. We were slumped on the sofa, eyes glued to the playback monitor as Walter ran through everything that had been shot.

"It looks good," I couldn't keep the bubble of enthusiasm from my voice. "The girls look incredible together, don't they?"

Walter nodded. He was passionate about his profession and constantly critical, but even he was smiling. "It's a good one," he agreed.

Connie came in from the sunlight with her notebook clutched tightly in her fingers. The pages were frayed and curling, filled with her flowing looping handwriting. She came to a halt when she saw us and her eyes flicked to the monitor. She watched without comment for several minutes as Walter replayed the come shot, then she turned her eyes to where we sat.

"You guys look like the three wise monkeys," she said, "hear no evil, see no evil and speak no evil."

For some reason, that amused her immensely. She gave a little chortle of laughter and then foraged in her handbag for a new notebook.

"I know you're not a film critic," I ignored the aspersion she cast. "But what did you think of the filming?"

Connie looked blank for a moment, but I could see there was a lot going on behind her eyes.

When she had assembled her thoughts, she inclined her head and then nodded. "It was more tasteful than the previous scenes you have filmed," she declared in a comment that could have been praise or could have been a criticism.

I shrugged and gestured with my hands. "What does that mean? Is that a good thing or a bad thing?"

"It's a good thing," Connie conceded. "I felt you were able to capture something more than just porn," she said. "Even I thought that was sexy."

I almost fell off the sofa. Maybe I was hear no evil – maybe I wasn't hearing her correctly.

"You thought that was sexy?" I was shocked.

"I did," Connie nodded, and then she blushed and became flustered, like maybe she had said too much. She turned her attention quickly back to whatever was in her handbag. I pushed myself up off the sofa and gave my camera guys both a hardy slap on the back.

"Nice work, guys."

I drifted down the hallway towards the bathroom. I needed a shower.

As I came level with one of the spare bedrooms, I noticed the door was slightly ajar, and I paused, reaching out for the handle to draw it closed.

From within the room beyond came the sound of sexy feminine giggles, and a voice made husky with emotion and broken by panting gasps of breath. I nudged the door open with my elbow and saw Becky and Lily on their hands and knees, naked on the bed. Spread out between them was Yvette. The young girl had her eyes closed and her legs spread wide with Becky and Lily hovering over her, taking turns to lick her pussy.

I watched for just a moment... no, I didn't. I watched for several minutes, and then reluctantly wandered into the bathroom.

Damn! Now I needed another cold shower.

Chapter 20.

It was late in the afternoon before the three actresses emerged from the bedroom. They were dressed and looked like they were going somewhere. They were.

With filming finished, the girls were no longer needed. We exchanged hugs and kisses and promises to stay in touch and made plans to film together again in the near future. My camera guys were on their way back to Europe, and I stood on the front step of the house as all five of them piled into a hired car and drove away.

When I came back inside, it was just Connie and I – alone in the house.

"Well," I said with a lazy smile. "Now that you have me all to yourself, whatever would you like to do with me?"

Connie flicked me a smile. "I'd like to ask you a question."

I looked disappointed. "Is it a personal question? Is it a sexy question?"

"It's a question about sex," Connie said flatly.

"Is it a question about you and me having sex?" (Okay, I had pushed it as far as I could).

Connie did the sensible thing – she ignored me. She opened up her notebook to a blank page, and then stared down at it like maybe the question had been written in invisible ink. "Why don't you make films that have a BDSM theme?" she asked. "That genre is very popular right now, you know?"

I put on my game face. "I do know BDSM is popular at the moment," I admitted. "But it's only popular with women, and only with women who read particular erotic novels. BDSM might seem like a new trend that is suddenly sweeping the world, but the reality is that BDSM is nothing new. And there's nothing new in porn either."

Connie looked a little surprised. "So there has always been porn films made for people who have an interest in bondage and discipline?"

"Of course," I said. I dropped down onto the sofa with a weary sigh. "Connie, there are porn films made to cater for every imaginable fetish – and that includes BDSM. However, the BDSM films that are made are generally filmed for a male audience because men are the ones who largely watch porn films."

"So you don't feel that the interest over recent years in BDSM would translate to something marketable you could film?"

I shook my head. "The phenomenon you are referring to is largely confined to women *readers*. I make my films for male *viewers*," I emphasized the words.

Connie scribbled in her notebook, and when she looked up she suddenly seemed to realize that it was getting dark. She looked around with a curious expression on her face as if to say 'where did the sun go'.

"Where did the sun go?" she asked.

I glanced over my shoulder and shrugged. "It's been a long day. Doesn't time fly when you're having sex."

Connie got to her feet and ran her fingers down over her bottom and thighs to smooth the wrinkles out of her skirt. Her eyes flicked away from me and suddenly she was glancing past my shoulder. She was checking her reflection in one of the windows.

"Are you coming to dinner with me? Or do you want to meet me at the restaurant?"

Connie glanced at her watch. "What time have you made the reservation for?"

"Seven," I said, and then made a mental note to book a table for seven o'clock as soon as I could discreetly get to a phone.

Connie glanced down at her wristwatch again, and I saw her lips move silently like she was talking to herself – working something out in her mind. Maybe she was calculating travelling time, or maybe she was calling me a jerk under her breath. I didn't know.

She looked up at last. "I'll meet you there," she decided. "It's called 'Still Water', right?"

I nodded. "It's on Seventh Street."

Chapter 21.

I was waiting in the restaurant parking lot when Connie arrived a few minutes before seven. She was wearing a white blouse and a red leather skirt, cut half-way up her thigh. She looked classy – in a sexy kind of way. She smiled a greeting and I took her arm and we walked together round the corner of the building, her high heels clipping on the pavement.

The 'Still Water' was one of those intimate, low-lit restaurants that love-lost guys take their girlfriends to when they propose.

There were no lights – the place was lit by thousands of candles flickering from fittings along the walls and twinkling on every table. There was a piano in a corner behind the reception counter where a grizzled little old man played show tunes and love songs with a kind of effortless ease that only comes from familiarity. He smiled at me from behind his spectacles as Connie and I stood waiting in the small foyer. I smiled back. The pianist took a discreet gulp of his martini and then launched into a tinkling rendition of '*My Heart Will Go On*'.

The maître d' drifted out of the shadows like he was gliding an inch above the carpet. I never saw his legs move. He was a thin man in his fifties, immaculately dressed in suit and tie. He had a crop of wavy, silvered hair and a pencil moustache. He ran his finger down the reservations register and chewed on his lip so that it looked like his moustache was crawling into the corner of his mouth. He stabbed the page suddenly with a stub of his finger and looked up with a dramatic 'ahh', like he had discovered the secret elixir of life. "There you are," he said. "Welcome, Mr. and Mrs. Cassidy."

I felt Connie go stiff beside me.

"We're not married," I explained, and then I patted my trouser pocket as if I had something there.

The maître d' caught the gesture and gave me a knowing wink. "Very good, sir," he inclined his head. "'Still Water' would like to present you with a complimentary bottle of champagne," and then he leaned close to me and gave me a conspiratorial nod. "Good luck," he whispered.

I nodded back. "I'll need it," I whispered. "I'm sure the bottle of champagne will help tremendously."

The maître d' gestured with his hands to suggest it was the least he could do for a couple deeply in love, on the brink of their proposal. He led us to a table and pulled Connie's chair out for her to sit. He bowed to me and smiled at Connie. "Enjoy your evening," his voice was soft and smooth. "Your complimentary champagne will be brought right out. Hopefully, by the end of this night, you will both have something wonderful to celebrate."

The maître d' disappeared back into the gloom. Connie looked a question at me. "Are you a regular here?"

I shook my head.

Connie frowned. "Strange," she mused. "The maître d' spoke to you like he knew you. I thought he might have been a fan of your films, and that's why we're getting the complimentary champagne."

I shook my head and shrugged with innocent wonder. "It's a mystery."

It was early evening, and many of the restaurant tables were empty, but reserved. I glanced past Connie's shoulder and saw a dozen other couples leaning close together over the intimate candlelit settings of their tables. There was a confidential hum of whispered conversation around the room. I heard a woman behind me chuckle in that throaty, sexy way that women do when they are aroused – or drunk. A man at the table across from us reached out and rubbed the forearm of the woman he was sitting opposite like he was trying to soothe her temper. The woman didn't respond.

"Have you ever watched people?" I asked Connie.

She frowned. "In what way?"

I flapped my hand. "Just watched them. Just sat somewhere and observed strangers – how they move, the gestures they make, the habits..."

Connie was still frowning. "I'm a journalist," she said, as if that answer was enough.

"So?"

"I'm trained to observe," she said. "I make a living writing about people, Rick. It has taught me to be a good observer."

I sat back and thought about that. "Then you must have plenty of observations to make about me."

"A notebook full," she said dramatically.

I sucked in a breath through my teeth. It made a little hissing sound. "So tell me," I invited. "Don't hold back."

Connie laughed lightly and glanced away for an instant. "You want me to tell you what I really think about you?"

"I do," I nodded and made the brave kind of face a man makes when he's being stood before a firing squad. "Blaze away."

Connie shook her head. "I won't do that."

"Why not?"

"Because..." Connie's voice dropped to a whisper so I could barely hear her.

I leaned forward across the table. "Because why?"

"Because you haven't paid for dinner yet."

(Beautiful *and* witty!)

"You can say whatever you feel, Connie," I encouraged her. "You may not think so, but I actually am a gentleman and I've got a pretty thick skin. I asked for your honesty, so please, be honest. Do I need to change my name and go into hiding once your article is published? Or should I buy a set of those plastic spectacles with a big rubber nose and moustache attached?"

Connie smiled and the warmth of it reached all the way to her eyes. "My story in '*Infinity*' won't be published for another month," she said.

"So?" I leaned across the table again.

"So by then, you could have a pair of breasts and go by the name of Gloria."

(Okay, now she was just being evil).

Not funny.

Connie's smile kept spreading. It turned up the corners of her mouth and became a playful grin. "Relax," she reached out and patted my arm. It was the first time she'd ever deliberately touched me and I felt the chilled shock of it. Her fingers were warm and delicate. "I think you will be pleasantly surprised when you read the published article."

I sat back, and I realized to the casual observer that all of my sudden leaning backwards and forwards probably made me look like I was in the grips of some uncontrollable spasm. "I'm shocked," I said, meaning it. "I thought you thought I was an ass."

"I do," Connie said. "But you have some redeeming qualities, Rick Cassidy – even for an ass."

A waiter arrived with an iron stand and a silver bucket. In the bucket was a bottle of champagne in a nest of ice. The waiter made an elaborate show of presenting the label to me and then popped the cork and missed the woman's head beside us by just an inch.

The waiter filled both our glasses and then backed away from the table in smooth effortless actions – until he dropped to the floor and crawled around to retrieve the cork.

Connie snatched up her glass and sipped at the champagne. "It's true," she sounded surprised. "The bubbles really do tickle your nose." She took another longer sip of champagne and set the glass down close by her hand. She looked at me and there was a glistening twinkle in her eye that hadn't been there a few moments earlier. She frowned for an instant, as though trying to recall where the conversation had left off.

"You are brash and arrogant and egotistical," Connie said without any venom at all. "Women treat you like you are some magnificent sex god. They throw themselves at you, and you love the adoration. But I understand that," Connie took another sip of champagne before she went on. "I understand that because it's part of the image you need to present for your work. But it's not the real you. Beneath everything you show yourself to be is the real Rick Cassidy. Not the porn star, I mean Rick, the man."

"Hell," I said. "You're starting to worry me."

Connie shook her head, shaking off my concern. "I told you not to worry," she said. "My article will be a glowing endorsement of your morals and ethics in an industry where so often those high standards you set are diminished or ignored completely. I intend to portray you as the dedicated professional that I believe you are."

And then she added like she was pronouncing the sentence, "I promise, the true Rick Cassidy will not be revealed."

"It sounds like you've got me all summed up," I said.

"The exterior façade, yes."

I looked intrigued. "You think there's more to me?"

"Much more," Connie said with feeling. She took another sip of champagne. The glass was almost empty. "I think you are a hopeless romantic," Connie declared. "I didn't think it was possible. When I first met you, I didn't think you had a caring sensitive bone in your big rippling body." She paused for a moment and her eyes fixed onto mine. "And then you told me about Amelia, the girl you loved and lost in Italy. In that short conversation I realized the real you is nothing like the image you show the world. Deep down, you're not happy because you're not in love. Rick Cassidy isn't ten foot tall and bulletproof. He is as vulnerable and as lonely and as lost in this life as the rest of us."

Ouch!

I reached for my champagne and emptied the glass. I snatched the bottle from the bucket and refilled my glass, then splashed a little more into Connie's glass. I sat there, stunned. I tried to keep my gaze expressionless, but I felt tiny cracks at the edges of my face. "You gained all that insight from one brief conversation we had about a girl I knew seven years ago?"

Connie said nothing. She just stared at me knowingly from over the rim of her champagne glass.

I caught sudden movement from the corner of my eye and the inept waiter who had almost decapitated the lady with the champagne cork came to the table, clutching two menus under his arms like they were the stone tablets Moses brought down from the mountain. He laid them out with great care on the table and stood there silently.

Maybe he was waiting for applause.

"I'll have steak," I said without looking at the menu.

"How would you like your steak cooked, sir?" the waiter asked in a sing-song voice.

"Burned," I said. "Tell the chef to cook it until he gets the shits."

The waiter looked confused. "Shits?"

I nodded. "It means I want the steak cooked until the chef is incensed about cremating a perfect piece of steak. Understand?"

The waiter nodded, but there was a grim look on his face like it was bad news he didn't want to bear. He turned his attention to Connie. "Madam?"

Connie flipped open the menu and ran her eyes in quick appraisal down the two pages of elegant script. She looked up and smiled sweetly. "I'll have the same," she said.

"A steak, madam?"

She nodded with a wicked glint. "Yes, that's right," she closed the menu and handed it back to the waiter. "And ask the chef to burn it for me."

The waiter froze. I saw him dart a glance over his shoulder to the kitchen. "Are you sure, madam?"

"With the fat trimmed off."

"Yes, madam," the waiter said reluctantly.

Connie nodded. "I like my steak the way I like my men – black and lean."

The waiter flinched. He looked aghast. He minced off towards the kitchen reluctantly.

"That was funny," I said. "I didn't realize you had a sense of humor."

Connie chuckled. "I've been dying to use a line like that ever since I saw the movie, '*Flying High*'." She sipped more of her champagne. A soft crimson flush of color was spreading across her cheeks and making her eyes sparkle in the candlelight. I watched her for a long moment and then I leaned across the table in the gloomy intimate light and dazzled Connie with my most charming smile.

"Have you thought more about my offer?"

She raised an eyebrow. "What offer?"

"Sex," I said, holding the smile until my face began to ache. "You and me in a big bed, all alone. Me covering your body with kisses as I slowly peel away your clothes. You, lying beneath me, writhing as my fingers and lips explore your breasts. My cock pressing against your thigh, you taking me in your hands..."

Connie sat back so her face was shadowed. She reached for her champagne.

"You don't want me because you want me, Rick."

Huh?

I shook my head. "What does that mean?"

Connie sighed like she wished it wasn't true. "You want me because you can't have me, that's all."

"Then let me have you."

She laughed, and maybe for the first time, it sounded genuine. "You want me because I am a challenge," Connie said. "You're used to every woman you meet willingly tumbling into bed with you. Then you meet me, and I'm not interested. That makes me a challenge – not an object of your desire."

"Maybe that's what makes you so desirable."

Connie sat forward, set her glass down and propped her elbows on the table, cupping her face in her hands and gazing into my eyes. "You certainly don't want me because of love... and you can't possibly want to have sex with me because of some lust you feel. Jesus, you have sex with so many women you can't possibly have that itch. It's not like you haven't laid eyes on a woman for six months."

"So? What are you getting at?"

"Your motive," she said simply. "You don't have a good reason for wanting to take me to bed, other than the fact that I represent some kind of a challenge to you – and so you only want me because you can't have me."

"Isn't that a good enough reason?" I scowled. "How many reasons does a guy need to want to have sex with a woman?"

Connie shrugged. "Then if you want sex, why not just go back to the house and fuck one of your actresses," she said bluntly. "They're younger than me, they're prettier than me. They're more experienced and more adventurous than me..."

"But I want you."

"Because you haven't had me."

"...Yet."

"And because you *can't* have me," Connie ignored my thrust.

Our meals arrived. The waiter placed our plates on the table before us and turned on his heel without a look or a word. Connie and I stared down at the table. Our steaks looked like pieces of charcoal that had been dragged from a fire, surrounded by a delicate sprinkle of shredded vegetables.

We ate in silence, and when the waiter next ghosted passed, I ordered a fresh bottle of champagne. Somewhere in the murky gloom, a young woman gasped and then squealed with delight. Heads turned and there was a smatter of applause. The young man seated opposite stood up and bowed.

"How would you go about getting more women to watch porn movies, Rick?" Connie's voice slurred at the edges of her words. She gazed at me with a fixed look in her eyes and leaned forward, frowning as though the question was something that had been troubling her deeply.

I sat back and thought about that for a moment. "First, I would change the name," I said.

"What do you mean?"

"Pornography," I said. "Porn. The fact is that the mention of the name comes with certain connotations, especially in the minds of women. They have the same preconceived notions that you had," I said frankly. "So the first step would be to start calling porn something else."

"But it would still be porn."

"Of course," I conceded. "But big companies often rebrand themselves to reach new markets. I would need some marketing wiz-kid to come up with a catchy name. That would be the first step."

Connie sipped at her champagne, then rested one elbow on the table and cupped her cheek in her hand. "Then what?"

"I guess I would need to change the type of men who I use in films," I frowned. "You see, right now the role of the man in a porn film is really quite secondary to the role of the actress. The guy is there to provide a long hard dick – and not much else. For a long time, the main requirement for a man in porn has been the size of his penis and his ability to get hard. If I was trying to reach a female audience I would need to start casting rugged, good-looking men, and spend more time filming them, rather than just focusing on the actress and the sex that takes place."

Connie nodded slowly. "Would that be difficult?"

I nodded. "Yes, actually. It would be difficult."

Connie looked fascinated, but some of that fascination could be attributed to the alcohol. She was drinking like a fish. "Why?" She smiled like she was thinking about something more important.

"Well, I can only think of one incredibly good looking guy with an amazing physique, rugged swarthy good looks and a phenomenal cock who can get hard and stay hard when required. And that's me," I joked.

Connie gazed at me. She didn't say anything. Maybe she hadn't heard.

I went on, "The truth is that there aren't that many good looking guys who also have the physical requirements to perform in porn. Most good looking guys only have average-size cocks, and most *really* good looking guys – the ones who groom and use product and wear expensive Italian suits – well, they're gay."

Connie stayed silent, and I wondered if I should tell her that I was only joking. She just gazed at me like she was hypnotized.

I leaned forward and touched her fingers. "Are you okay?"

Connie blinked and her eyes slowly came into some kind of focus. She smiled, but it was one of those languid smiles that just slipped straight back off her lips. She widened her eyes like she had seen something frightening. "I'm fine," she said in a soft daze. "I'm just enjoying listening to the sound of your voice."

"You're drunk."

Connie sat upright suddenly. "I am not!" she said defensively.

I set my wine glass down on the table. "I think it might be time for us to go home."

Connie drained the champagne in the bottom of her glass. She stood up, and then teetered. She made a grab for the edge of the table, and smiled at me self-consciously. "New heels," she said. "I'm still getting used to them."

I nodded. "You're drunk."

I took Connie by the elbow and guided her carefully out of the restaurant. The maître d' took my money and bid us a pleasant evening. He gave me a smarmy smile and wrung his hands together.

We stepped outside into the warmth of the evening, the frenetic sounds of the city swelling all around us. The sidewalks were crowded with pedestrians, the streets choked with cabs and cars, and the buzz of nightlife. I put my arm around Connie's shoulder and steered her towards the parking lot. I got her into the passenger seat of my car and revved the engine.

"You're coming home with me," I said, my voice flat and devoid of any emotion. "You can stay at my place tonight. There is no way I'm letting you drive home in your condition, so don't even try to argue with me," I insisted. "I won't be responsible for you getting behind the wheel – and I don't care what you say."

Connie said nothing.

I pulled out of the parking lot and wedged the car into the snaking line of traffic. I glanced across at Connie. She was asleep.

Chapter 22.

We lurched through the front door. Connie stood swaying on her feet, like she was on the deck of a ship in a rising storm. I propped her up against the wall while I went through the house, flicking on lights. Connie started to sag forward from the waist and I caught her before she dropped to the floor. I wrapped my arm around her and steered her down the hallway to the main bedroom. She sat on the edge of the bed and then flopped backwards as though her body had lost all its strength. Her eyes were open, gazing at something unseen and out of focus on the ceiling. There was a grin on her lips, but at the same time she was frowning, as though the effort making herself smile took fierce concentration.

I got onto the bed beside her and unbuttoned Connie's blouse. The silk fell open and I reached with one hand beneath her to unfasten the clasp of her bra. Connie rolled her head and slapped limply at my hand. "Hey," she muttered drunkenly. "Don't touch the merchandise."

Her blouse and bra came off. Her body was slim, her breasts large and retaining their shape. There was a soft peppering of freckles across her chest, set against the pale smooth skin of her cleavage.

I unbuckled the straps of her shoes and then wriggled her skirt and panties off. Connie lay completely naked, and under the soft golden glow of the bedroom lights she looked toned and fit and very feminine. Her body was mature, with a womanly weight to her breasts and hips, but I could still make out the rack of her ribs beneath the skin. There was a wispy tuft of fine hair at the base of her belly. Connie groaned and then buried her fingers in the bed sheets with dulled urgency.

"Everything is moving," she slurred the words. "Make it stop!"

I got undressed and pulled the covers over us. Connie rolled onto her side and threw her arm across my chest as though I was an anchor she could cling to in order to stop the bed from swaying. I lay on my back with my hand thrust beneath my head, staring at a patch of moonlight on the wall.

Connie began to softly snore.

Chapter 23.

I woke up with Connie's cheek buried in the crook of my neck, her soft warm breath tickling the hairs on my chest. I was lying on my back, and she was lying on her side, curled up around me. She had one arm draped across my waist and one of her legs thrown over mine. My arm was numb.

Connie stirred tentatively, then moaned. Her eyes fluttered open and she did that thing that ladies sometimes do when they wake up in a strange bed in a strange house in the arms of a strange man.

She screamed.

"What the fuck?"

She sat bolt upright in the bed. The sheets fell down around her waist so that her breasts bounced. She stared at me, wide eyed with her mouth hanging open, slack in shock and horror.

Then glanced down at herself and realized she was naked.

Then she realized I was naked too.

She clutched at the sheets and heaved them up to modestly cover herself. Her face was pale and bloodless. She glared at me with a ferocious look.

"You... you... fucking..."

I yawned. "Good morning."

Connie went ballistic. "Don't you fucking good morning me, you bastard," she hissed. She was trembling with rage. Beneath the clutch of the bed sheets I could see her breasts rising and falling with every angry breath.

"Don't tell me we..." she began and then cut herself off as though the possibility was just too horrible to utter the words. "We didn't – did we?"

I propped myself up onto one elbow and stared at her with a look of wide-eyed innocence. "Did what?"

"You know damn well what!" Connie snapped.

I shook my head. "I'm sorry. I don't know what you mean."

There was a blaze of fire behind Connie's eyes, yet her lips were drawn into an ice-cold grimace. "Sex," she hissed. "Did you take advantage of me last night and use me for your sexual pleasure?"

"Sex?" I said the word like I'd never heard it before in my life.

She punched me – *and it fucking hurt.*

"Don't fuck with me!" she raged.

"According to you, I already have."

Connie shook her head like this was some horrible nightmare. Her dark tousled hair swished across her shoulders. "Oh, god no!"

I swung my legs off the bed and stood up. I was naked. I stared at Connie. "Relax," I said gently. "You were drunk. I brought you home because I didn't want you driving. I undressed you and put you into bed – *and nothing happened.*"

Connie huffed in disbelief. She was still simmering with rage. "You undressed me – or tore my clothes off to have your way with me?"

"I undressed you," I said flatly. "And then carefully folded your clothes and put them at the foot of the bed. Not too many guys I know would rip off a woman's clothes and then go to the trouble of folding them neatly for her."

Connie lost a little of her bluster. "How do I know you didn't take advantage of me?"

I smiled. "Stand up," I said. "If you can walk — then we didn't have sex."

Chapter 24.

I burned eggs and then I burned toast before settling for a glass of bourbon. I switched on the television to catch the morning news. The announcer said, "And now to a developing story in Japan..." as Connie appeared in the hallway, dressed in the clothes she had worn the night before. Her hair looked more brown than black in the bright sunlight, and it was disheveled. She had washed her face of make-up and her face looked like a child's, but her body language read otherwise. She strode across to the television. I had been sipping at my bourbon. The glass was almost empty.

"Are you watching this?" she asked softly.

I shook my head.

Connie switched the TV off and stood to position herself in my line of sight. "I'd like to talk to you."

I nodded. "Go ahead."

But she didn't. She didn't say anything for a long time. Instead she went to the kitchen, saw the mess I had made, and decided that breakfast was a meal she could skip. She came back into the living room and sat beside me on the sofa whilst smoke swirled in lingering tendrils below the ceiling.

Outside the morning had dawned warm and sunny. Through the windows I could see the haze of city smog turning the rim of the horizon soft and grey.

(Or it might have been smoke from the eggs and toast).

Connie sat pensive and thoughtful, her head bowed, kneading her fingers with some tension that lurked just below the surface. I glanced at her over the rim of my glass as I drank.

"Do you think you have enough for your article?" I asked. My voice was brisk and bright, like I didn't know Connie had things on her mind.

She looked up at me, and it seemed to take a second for the question to register.

"Um... yes," she said finally. "I think I have all that I need."

"Last day here in L.A.," I said like a warning. "So if there's anything — anything at all that's been left unanswered, now is the time to ask."

That seemed to trigger another wave of dark brooding. Connie lapsed into silence and I sat waiting patiently.

"I'm sorry about this morning," she said at last, her voice subdued. "I overreacted."

This wasn't it. This wasn't what was on her mind, but at least she was talking.

I shrugged off her apology. "That's okay," I said. "I guess I can understand you feeling the way you felt and thinking what you thought, given what you have seen of me over the past few days."

She shook her head. "No," she said, "I've seen enough of you so that I should have known better. I shouldn't have jumped to the conclusion that I did and... and I'm grateful to you — for bringing me back here and not letting me drive." She blushed as she spoke.

"How's your head?"

"Pounding."

"You drank a lot of champagne in a short amount of time."

She smiled wryly – an expression of remorse and regret. "I don't know how you do it," she said, shaking her head slowly and looking into my eyes. "I don't know how you can drink so much alcohol and never feel hung over." She waved her hand in the air, gesturing at the bourbon I was nursing. "Even now," her voice rose a little. "You're drinking alcohol for breakfast."

I leaned close to her as though to share a secret. Our shoulders brushed. "I have a technique," I intimated. "The only way to drink as much as I do and not feel hung over is to stay drunk."

Connie looked at me with one of those pained expressions I had seen on her face so many times before. It was the face she wore whenever I was sarcastic.

"I'll keep that in mind," she said dryly and then lapsed back into dark silence.

I pushed myself to my feet and went around the kitchen cleaning up. I threw the frying pan, the eggs and the toast into the trash bin, then stared down thoughtfully for a moment at my empty glass.

Was there a dishwasher somewhere?

I stood holding the glass for a moment, and then re-filled it.

Problem solved.

Connie was watching me closely – we made eye contact.

"Rick..." Connie said suddenly in the kind of voice that precedes an explosive question, "I have something to ask you, and it's serious."

I braced myself. "I thought all your questions had been serious."

"They have," she smiled thinly. "But this one is more serious... because it's about us."

"Us?" I was genuinely surprised. "I didn't know there was an 'us'."

"I mean it's not about your work. It's a personal question."

Now I was intrigued. I went back into the living room and sat down in the big leather chair near the front door.

(in case I needed a quick escape).

"Go on..." I said warily.

Connie made a face like she was trying to find the right words. She pouted, sighed, looked away... and then turned her head back and stared into my eyes. They were glistening.

"If I had sex with you, would you do me a favor?"

"No."

She frowned. "No?"

"No," I said again. I got to my feet and sighed. "Connie, if you need a favor then ask. I'll do it — and you don't have to sleep with me."

"But you don't know what the favor is," she protested. "And you told me that this industry was a network of favors and payback."

I shrugged. "I don't care. If I can help you, I will."

"Just like that?"

"Just like that."

"And you wouldn't want me to pay you back? You wouldn't hold it over my head like a debt owed?"

"No."

"Why?"

"Because I like you."

She smiled, and then her eyes misted up and her lip began to tremble. She sniffed, then said softly, "That makes me want to sleep with you."

I shook my head. "What does?"

"The fact that you would do me a favor after the way I have been since I first met you."

"You're a total contradiction," I agreed pointedly. "Everything you have said from the moment we met has been anti-porn... and now you're talking about having sex with me."

She nodded, and then shook her head in exactly the kind of contradiction that had been the source of my frustration. "I have been anti-porn," she admitted. "But I don't hate you."

"Well you could have fooled me."

She huffed wryly. "I tried to fool myself," she said softly. "But what I have been saying about... your work... isn't what I have been thinking and feeling..."

"Meaning?"

She shrugged her shoulders, like it should be obvious. "Meaning that despite my best efforts to hate you, I actually like you," she said. "You're a good man – not the kind of man I expected you to be."

I said nothing.

Connie began pacing the floor, making small gestures with her hands and frowning as though she was holding a conversation with herself. Finally she took a deep shuddering breath and gave me a smile that made her lips tremble. She was nervous.

"I would very much like to have sex with you," she said in a gush of breath.

I stared at her for long considering seconds. "You don't mean that."

She nodded. "I do, actually," she said. "But not because you're some famous porn star – I'm certainly not a giddy groupie," she smiled thinly. "I want to sleep with you because I like you, because I'll probably never see you again, and because beneath the brash abrasive exterior I think you're a kind and considerate man."

I shook my head slowly. "Connie, don't do this because you want to ask me a favor. I have already told you that I will do what I can to help you. You don't have to sleep with me – this shouldn't be about some kind of payback."

"It isn't," Connie said. She came a couple of steps closer. She was shaking like a leaf. She looked like she was on the verge of tears. Her bottom lip quivered. She gazed into my eyes. "I want this," she said.

I took her hand, and there was a spark of something electric in her touch. "If we do this," I said seriously, "we do it simply because you want to and I want to – with no strings attached. But regardless, I will do the favor that you ask of me. Just tell me what it is."

Connie shook her head. "Later," she said softly and then she raised herself onto tiptoes and brushed her lips across mine. I stood like a statue.

Connie leaned back and searched my eyes. There was a hectic flush of color on her cheeks and her breathing was sharp and unsteady. She kissed me again and her mouth moved sensually over mine as I felt the warmth of her body press against me. I felt the moist flicker of her tongue and my lips parted as the kiss filled with passion and then hunger. Connie moaned – the sound coming from somewhere deep in her chest and I felt the vibration of it like little ripples of lust as her arms entwined around my neck.

I deepened the kiss. My hands went around Connie's waist and she arched her back, submitting to the force of me. I could smell the lingering scent of her perfume and the womanly muskiness of her body. I could feel the tremors of her apprehension.

I broke the kiss. Connie was panting, each breath moving her breasts below the silk of her blouse.

"Are you sure?" I asked one last time. "Connie, we don't have to do this."

"I'm sure," her eyes sparkled and there was something definite in the tone of those two words.

I took Connie's hand and we drifted into the bedroom.

Chapter 25.

The drapes were pulled tight across the big windows, muting the light in the room and blocking out the glare of sunshine. The room was warm, the bed still dented with the impressions of our bodies and where we had slept. I turned to Connie at the foot of the bed and held her at arms length.

"You can say no right now and I will understand completely," I said. "I won't hate you for leading me on, and we can walk back out of this bedroom as friends, right now, if that's what you want."

Connie lunged for me impulsively, bringing her body within the circle of my arms and capturing my face in the palms of her hands. She pulled my lips down to hers and kissed me fiercely.

"You talk too much," she breathed. Her breath was warm and soft. She kissed me again and my arms seemed to act without command, wrapping themselves around her tiny waist and crushing her pelvis against the hardness that was swelling in my jeans. Connie's hands played down the length of my spine, pricking me with her nails, goading my flesh and setting me on fire.

My hands roamed over the firmness of her bottom, gliding over the leather of her skirt and reaching down towards the hem. Connie rocked her body against mine in a rhythm that became an erotic grinding dance. She undulated, so that one moment I felt the firm jutting press of her breasts and then the next the push of her hips and thighs.

My fingers tickled the hem of her skirt and then tugged at it. I bunched the fabric high up on her thigh and then reached down for the cleft of heat between her legs, skimming the palm of my hand over the satin of her panties.

Connie groaned a throaty murmur of encouragement as my fingers brushed across the molten dampness of her sex.

She plucked at the buttons of my shirt, peeling it off my shoulders and then rubbing the palms of her hands across the contours of my chest muscles and digging her thumbs into the taut flesh of my shoulders. Her touch was like fire, igniting fresh sparks of electric desire that I felt as a fierce and sudden clench like a gripping fist in my loins. Connie cooed. "Hmmm," she gasped seductively. "You're hard."

"Very," I grunted. I stretched out my fingers until I could press the fabric of her panties into the folds of her pussy. "I want you."

Connie's hands travelled over the broad of my chest and down over my torso as if her fingertips were reading the rippled contours of my body like brail. She unfastened the button on my jeans and tugged the zipper down. My pants gaped open and she reached inside with both hands and cupped the hard heat of my erection.

"Fuck," she whispered softly, as if to herself.

I sucked in a hiss of breath, the feel of her grip making me pulse and leap to life. There was a sudden scared and uncertain flicker across Connie's eyes. "It's so big," she breathed. "I... I..."

I covered her mouth with a kiss, stifling the words on her lips and the clench of sudden tension in Connie's body dissolved. The energy transferring to smoldering heat. She swayed in my arms and shuffled her feet apart. I hooked my thumb into the elastic waistband of her panties and drew them down her thighs. We were locked together, kisses burning on our lips. I felt Connie's hands free me from my jeans and then begin to stroke me.

I snatched at the buttons of her blouse. It was wispy shimmering fabric that seemed to drift open like a curtain, revealing the bulging swell of firm milky cleavage. I let the garment fall to the ground and unsnapped the clasp of her bra.

Connie's breasts were large – almost too large for the petite narrow frame of her body. I cupped the fleshy weight of one into the palm of my hand and lowered my mouth onto her nipple.

"Oh, I love that," Connie groaned through clenched teeth. I felt her grip on my cock tighten to a squeeze and then become a flurry of quick teasing strokes.

Somehow she got one of her hands to the nape of my neck, holding my mouth fiercely against her breast and arching her back at the same time as if to thrust herself into my mouth. My lips plucked at the rosy pink nub of her, drawing and tugging and teasing so that she gasped and writhed within my arms.

"The bed," she moaned. "I can't wait any longer."

Without breaking free from each other we fell onto the bed in a tangle of clinging arms. Connie rolled onto her back and I moved myself on top of her. Her legs fell wide open and I covered her throat and neck with kisses.

My jeans fell away, Connie's skirt was bunched up around her hips. I felt the press of my cock jutting between her thighs and then the sensation of sudden slick dampness as I brushed against her sex.

Connie went suddenly rigid, and I held myself poised there on the brink for several seconds. My cock was pulsing and Connie held her legs tensed and flexed. I raised myself up onto my elbows, braced above her with our torsos pressed together and stared down into her eyes.

"Take me," she whispered.

I tilted my hips and the swollen head of me pushed itself just an inch or two inside Connie's pussy.

She was seized in a sudden rictus of sensations. Her breath choked in the back of her throat and I saw her eyes fly wide in astonishment. She grunted at last as I held myself at the breach of her depths, letting her body become accustomed. For long moments neither of us moved. I felt Connie's fingertips play across my hips, fluttering as though trying to grip at my flesh. I felt the sudden flood of her arousal and I pushed myself more deeply inside, watching the gentle rock and sway of her breasts as she lay like a sacrifice beneath me.

Connie trapped her bottom lip between her teeth. She closed her eyes, lost in concentration. I sank deeper into her pussy and then paused once more as my cock reflexively began to throb and the sheath of Connie's sex gripped and rippled around me.

"More?" I asked gently.

Connie nodded her head. "Yes," she gasped.

I filled her with one long slow final thrust. Connie heaved herself up and threw her arms around my neck so that my elbows collapsed and my chest pressed against her breasts. She kissed me with a sudden maddened desire and then hooked her ankles over the backs of my legs so that our bodies were wrapped together in the timeless rhythm of intimacy.

We rocked together in the gentle deliberate rhythm of a boat on a calm sea, riding the long rolling swells as our passions ebbed and flowed. Connie felt delicate and fragile beneath me, and yet her body moved with a hunger and a lust that more than matched my own. She was veracious. She thrust her tongue into my mouth and dug her fingers into my butt, as if to draw me more deeply inside her.

I buried my face in the crook of her neck, hearing the soft whimpering sounds of her pleasure, and then kissed the soft pale flesh of her throat as our bodies drove themselves remorselessly on and on. There was a glisten of perspiration on Connie's brow and across her chest. As the heat from our bodies seemed to fuse our flesh together, she cried out suddenly and then her head thrashed on the pillow as she reached the brink of an orgasm and plummeted over the precipice.

I held myself perfectly still, my cock deep and tight inside her as Connie's body shuddered and spasmed and her hips thrust back at me as if she hungered for more. Ragged pants of breath exploded across her lips and the sudden pleasure of her release spilled across her face.

Silence.

Uncertain hectic breathing.

I rolled carefully off Connie and lay beside her. I put a tender hand over her heart and felt the racing thump of it as though it might burst from the cage of her chest. There was a crimson flush of color across her chest. Her eyes flickered, hazed and misty with distance. Her legs were splayed and limp. She had one hand pressed down on the mound of her sex as though something had changed there within her. I drew the tip of my finger in a slow searching line down across her abdomen towards where her hand rested.

"Are you okay?" I asked softly.

Connie nodded and there was a soft hum in the back of her throat before she spoke. "You made me come," she said as though it was a source of astonishment and wonder to her.

I smiled lazily. "That was the idea."

She smiled despite herself but then shook her head as though I didn't understand. "You don't understand," she said. "I've never..."

"Never?"

"Never," she said. "Not with a man. Only when I have been alone."

I looked suddenly surprised. "*Never?*" I had to ask again.

"You're the first."

I rolled onto my back. My cock jutted upright, thrusting at the ceiling. I felt Connie's hand creep across my thigh, her fingertips feeling like the soft tingling touch of spider's legs. "I need to find a way to pay you back," she smiled coyly.

"I can think of several," I grinned. She raised herself up onto her hands and knees and moved her body until her mouth was poised and open over the twitching head of my cock. I could feel the hot breeze of her breath. Connie licked her lips and gave me one last lingering sultry gaze before taking me into the moist embrace of her mouth.

She had no rhythm. Connie glided her lips up and down the slick glistening length of my shaft but the movement of her head was erratic and without any steady pace. At first I thought her inexperienced, but as the tingling sensations along the length of my shaft and deep inside me began to rise, I began to appreciate the immense skill she exerted. I found myself anticipating the next plunge of her mouth. I found myself tensing and lifting my hips from the bed, trying to keep the grip of her lips around my shaft. I felt my fists grip the edge of the bed and I clenched my jaw until my teeth began to ache. Connie played me like an instrument in the hands of a virtuoso. I felt the flickering sensation of pleasure suddenly ignite into a fire of exquisite painful expectation.

She wrapped her delicate fingers around the base of my cock and blew hot breath across my shaft like she was trying to extinguish a fire. "You like that?" she crooned.

"You're killing me," I grunted. "I'm close…"

A slow lazy smile of pleasure spread across Connie's face. She licked her lips lasciviously as though enjoying the taste of me. "Would you like to come?"

I grunted again and felt my toes curl, flexing the muscles in my calves and in my thighs. "Inside you," I said. "I want to come inside you."

Connie rolled onto her side, facing away from me and I rolled over so that we were spooned together. I wrapped my arm around her waist and reached up to cup her breast. Connie lifted her upper leg and then reached down between us and pressed the throbbing crown of my cock against the flared open entrance of her pussy.

I thrust inside her. Connie stiffened for an instant and then her whole body seemed to melt like wax. She went soft in my arms. She lowered her leg and we began to buck against each other as the tightness of her body served to grip and goad me until I knew I was about to burst.

I could smell the shampoo of Connie's hair. I inhaled the scents of sex that seemed to drift like smoke from her body. She pushed herself back against me with eagerness and then a long soft moan of throaty desire spilled from her lips.

"I'm going to come again," her voice was strained. "I don't believe this."

"Come with me!" I rasped, feeling the growing tension in Connie's body enhance and magnify my own racing need.

Our lovemaking lost all the gentle beauty of an erotic dance and instead became a desperate frantic need for our own releases. Our bodies crashed together. Connie's hands flailed and clawed. I felt my aching burn to explode override the last vestiges of tenderness and I plunged

myself deeper and harder within her until at last
– at long last – my body released and the ferocity
of my orgasm exploded behind my eyes. I felt
myself falling, spinning and spiraling down into
darkness. Connie was there too. She was gasping
and thrashing her body against me and we clung
together like survivors of an awesome tempest
until the storm passed and left us exhausted and
entwined on a bed of tangled sheets.

For many minutes neither of us spoke – we
were both overcome and completely spent. We
stared at each other, neither of us able to find the
words – neither of us knowing what words to say.
I was shattered. Connie's body rippled with the
aftershocks of her orgasm. She stared into space,
not seeing anything – seeing it all behind her eyes.

I moved like a man who had been washed
ashore in a storm. I rolled away, my limbs leaden
and heavy, my body weary. I propped myself up
on one elbow, lying on my side. I stared at Connie
stretched out on her back on the bed beside me.
We were both breathing raggedly. My chest was
glistening with the sweat of exertion. Connie's
eyes were closed and there was a soft smile of
deep satisfaction spread across her face. She had
one arm thrown across her breasts as though to
feel herself breathing. Her hair was tousled, the
bed sheets twisted beneath us. She lay perfectly
still.

"So..." I asked slowly, "... what's this favor you
wanted to ask me?"

Connie's eyes came open slowly as though she
were waking from a pleasant dream. She licked

dry lips, then turned her head to look up into my eyes.

"Later," she said softly. "I'm waiting for a phone call."

One of her hands reached out and she brushed her fingers across my torso in some innately feminine gesture as if to convince herself that I was real – that this hadn't been a fantasy. Her fingers lingered and then drifted lower, her intimate touch becoming almost possessive. She took my softening shaft gently in her hand with dreamy wantonness. "Thank you," she said.

I frowned. "You were my pleasure," I grinned.

Connie shook her head. "No, I mean thank you for not turning what we just shared into some gaudy scene from one of your films. I appreciate the fact that you made love to me – not just tried to use me for sex."

The smile stayed on my face but the emotion behind it became more serious and deeper. "You're a very easy lady to love like that," I said.

Then – as if on cue – Connie's cell phone began to trill from the living room... sounding like an alarm.

Chapter 26.

Connie flung herself from the bed and dashed on shaky legs and naked down the hallway. I dressed slowly, taking my time. I could hear snatches of Connie's response to the caller.

"What?" I heard her say in a stunned, shocked voice and then after a brief pause she said, "I thought I had more time."

When I could delay no longer I wandered into the living room. I had Connie's blouse and skirt in my hand. I held them out to her but she ignored me. She was standing, leaning against the wall with one arm folded across her chest, phone pressed hard against her ear, and she was facing away from me so that I could clearly see the raised little knuckles of her spine, and the seductive and very feminine flare of her waist and hips.

"Jesus!" Connie spat. She slapped a hand across her forehead and then shook her head as though everything in the world had gone horribly wrong.

I heard her mutter a soft, "thank you," that sounded like she didn't mean it, and then she ended the call.

She turned to me, her face was pale, her eyes wide and stricken. There was some appalling tension in her expression. Her mouth fell open as though there were words seized somewhere deep in her chest.

"What's wrong?" I went to her. I put my hands on her shoulders and stared into her eyes. "Tell me what's the matter, Connie."

It was like she forgot to breathe – or couldn't. She just stood there, darkness behind her eyes for long seconds, and then everything that had been locked up inside her escaped in a sudden ragged rush.

"The favor," she gasped. "Rick, I need your help, and I need it now."

I frowned. "Right now?"

Connie nodded her head vehemently. "Now, or I'm afraid it will be too late," she said and her voice was laced with dread.

I nodded. "Alright," I said. "What do you need me to do?"

Connie forced herself to snatch three settling breaths, the last one sounding like a forlorn sigh. "I need you to come with me. No questions asked," she said. "I just need you to trust me – and we need to go now."

Chapter 27.

I drove quickly, heading down in the hum of the city through a gauze of fumes, smog, and traffic noise. Connie had her phone in her hand, barking directions from a little map that displayed on the screen. It was late enough to have missed the early morning traffic jams, and too early for the crush of lunch break congestion, so we made good time racing between sets of traffic lights.

"Where are we going?" I asked.

"Turn left," Connie stabbed a finger at the windshield. I took the next turn and a flash of morning sunlight filled the car from a gap through the buildings that towered high on either side of the road.

"Where are we going?" I asked again. I stole a glance at Connie. She was frowning with complete concentration, clutching the phone in her hand like it was a precious missing fragment of the Dead Sea Scrolls.

"San Fernando."

"Can you be more specific?"

"Not until we get there," she said it in a tone that was ominous. "Take the next left."

I followed her directions and swung the car across traffic, heading deeper into the bowl of the valley.

"Then at least tell me why we are going where you can't tell me we are going."

That little piece of gibberish made her glance at me sharply. Her face was pinched and drawn with tight apprehension. Her eyes flicked back to the screen and she must of decided that she had time to spare before barking out the next direction. She sighed heavily. "My daughter," she said, like that explained everything.

I was shocked. "You have a daughter?"

Connie nodded. She glanced back down at the screen then across to me once more. "She's nineteen," Connie said. "She shares a house with a girlfriend of hers."

"And we're going to her house?"

"No," Connie shook her head but said no more. She peered through the windshield for several seconds and then her face registered some kind of recognition. "You need to change lanes," she said. "We have to turn right at the next set of lights."

I dutifully followed her instructions. The lights turned to red and I braked in a snarl of traffic.

"Then where are we going?"

"A place in the valley," Connie said. "That's where my daughter is."

Talking to Connie like this was like pulling teeth during interrogation. I felt like I was working her over the way cops do when they are prying information from a shady suspect. "Is your daughter in trouble?"

Connie nodded. "I think so."

The lights changed to green. "My daughter's name is Roxy," Connie said softly. "Her and I don't get along," she shrugged her shoulders as if to tell me that she didn't know why that was. "She moved out of home about eighteen months ago, and she has been living with a girlfriend in the valley ever since."

"What does she do? I mean, what does she do for a living?"

Connie grunted like she had been punched in the chest. "She is about to appear in her first porn film."

Aaah...

I said nothing, but behind my eyes everything was beginning to fall into place. I had a sudden sense of motivation behind Connie's vehement objection to the industry when she had first arrived for the interview.

"About a month ago, Roxy met a guy who said he was a modeling agent who happened to be scouting local nightclubs looking for girls who had the potential to be a star," Connie said in a flat voice. Then she turned her head to me and there was a weak watery smile on her lips. "Sound familiar?"

I nodded – but I said nothing, and with my silence I encouraged Connie to continue.

"This guy – he told Roxy that she could make a lot of money performing in adult movies. He told her he auditioned several girls a week and that she was someone special."

I grunted. I felt my fingers tightening on the wheel. "How do you know all this?"

Connie's wan smile faded away. "The girl she lives with," Connie explained. "She's the one who phoned me back at your house to tell me that Roxy's audition was happening today. We have been in touch over the past few weeks because her friend is as concerned as I am."

"She's a good friend indeed."

"I think so," Connie said and then lapsed into worried silence.

We were heading into a rundown decrepit part of the city. The high glimmering skyscrapers and vibrant bustle of the city began to give way to older derelict neighborhoods filled with abandoned buildings splashed in graffiti colors. The traffic thinned, and I stomped my foot down on the gas pedal.

"Second left," Connie said. For some inexplicable reason, she felt the need to point and curl her fingers at the same time as though maybe I wasn't sure which way left was.

"What do you expect from me?" I asked.

I stole another quick glance at Connie's face. Her eyes sparkled with brimming tears. "I just want you to talk to her, Rick," she said softly. "I just want you to be you. Tell her what she needs to know. That's all I ask."

I nodded... and then put an edge to my voice. "Is this why you hate the porn industry? Is this why you were so resentful when you first arrived to interview me?"

Connie shrugged her shoulders and then glanced at me with a look like she had been caught with her hand in the cookie jar. "Yes," she said. "I'm sorry. When I found out that Roxy was being coerced by this man to make a porn film, I got angry," she said. "And when the opportunity arose to interview someone from the porn industry, I saw it as my last chance to understand – or maybe to try to make Roxy understand. When I met you, I didn't hate you. I hated that my daughter was being preyed upon."

I took the turn and then slowed to a crawl. We were on a narrow grimy suburban street. Run-down buildings lined the litter-strewn sidewalk. Old beat-up cars were parked at haphazard angles along the curb. At the end of the street, I saw a young girl in ragged clothes pushing a stroller.

"This is it!" Connie said urgently. "This is where she is being filmed."

We found the building and I parked. I sat for a moment, staring across at Connie. Muted sounds of base-thumping music filled the air outside the car.

"What do you want me to do?" I asked again.

Connie turned to me. She reached for my hand and the grip of her fingers were fierce. "She's a good girl, Rick. She's my daughter. She is the only good thing that came from a brief and terrible marriage a long time ago. She's still a teenager – she doesn't know what the world is like. She's doing this..." Connie shook her head uncertainly, "... she's doing this to punish me, or maybe to show me that she's her own woman with her own mind capable of making her own decisions." The air seemed to go out of Connie like she was suddenly drained or exhausted. She sighed one last long breath and squeezed my fingers. "I just want you to talk to her."

We got out of the car and Connie took my hand and led me to a doorway. She was anxious, bristling with wrought nerves and tension. Her eyes searched mine.

"Please say you'll help me."

I nodded. "I'll help you."

We went in through the door and I stood in a dingy narrow hallway. There was water-stained wallpaper peeling off the walls and a riot of graffiti sprayed over an opposite doorway. The room smelled of urine and decomposition. I crossed the hall, pushed open the door – and stood there with Connie close at my side. The room was large. There were windows along one wall. Several panes of glass were broken and the rest were hazed in a film of thick dust so that the light was gloomy and dull. The room was large – like maybe it had once been a reception area or foyer for some kind of business. The floor was covered with old newspapers and in the far corner of the room a young woman was on her back, laying on a stained rumpled mattress set down on the hard floor. Kneeling between her spread legs was an overweight man, maybe fifty. He was naked. There was a thick pelt of dark hair matted across his chest and across the broad of his back. His face was pinched and seedy, and he was sweating profusely. The stink of him mingled with a swirl of stale cigarette smoke and hung thick in the air. The man had a small hand-held camera up to his eye as he plunged himself in and out of the girl's pussy.

Sitting on the floor nearby, knees tucked to her chin, arms hugged tightly around her legs, was a pretty young girl with enormous eyes set into an attractive pale face. The girl had long dark hair that hung past her shoulders. She was staring at the man as he rutted into the girl on the mattress in a series of oily obese lunges.

The pretty girl's head turned slowly towards me.

"My daughter," Connie said with a heartbreaking expression of torture on her face. "That's Roxy."

"Who's the other girl? Who's the one on the bed?"

Connie shook her head. She didn't know.

The man on the mattress was grunting. I could hear the girl's breath choking in her throat as she lay beneath him like she was made of stone. Her eyes were screwed tightly shut and she was biting on her bottom lip. I could see the loathing and sense of violation etched into the grimace of her expression. The man leered down at the girl.

"That's it, you horny slut," the man grunted. His lips were slack with desire, exposing a mouthful of bad teeth, and there was a froth of spittle on his lips. "Keep that tight little snatch of yours nice and wet for me until I'm ready to come."

I had seen enough.

"Go and get Roxy," I said.

I strode across the room and as I crossed the floor, the man suddenly turned his head and his eyes were wide with shock and then astonishment and then finally outrage and confusion. "What the fuck –!"

I reached down and fisted a handful of wiry coarse hair. The man shrieked like a girl. I heaved him to his feet. There was a simmer of red rage behind my eyes. The guy stank of sweat and alcohol – the odor wrinkling in my nostrils. I glared at him, thin lipped with fury. "Let the girls go," I hissed.

The guys face became swollen and contorted with defiance, and then an instant later it melted away. "Hey!" the guy said suddenly, and I caught a whiff of his rank fetid breath. "You're Rick fucking Cassidy! Jesus, you're Rick fucking Cassidy!"

I nodded. "I know," I said. "Who the fuck are you?"

The man suddenly thrust his hand out at me, his face alight and giddy. "Man, it's an absolute fucking honor to meet you. You're a legend, an absolute legend," he gushed. "My name is Jimmy D." I ignored his hand. I let go of the handful of hair I held and thumped the man in the middle of his chest with the point of my finger.

"You're finished with these girls," I said suppressing my rage just enough to snarl the words. "Have you touched the young one yet?"

The guy's head swung to where Connie was kneeling beside her daughter. The guy shook his head. "Not yet," he said. "But she signed a waiver."

I felt my hands clench into tight fists. "Get it," I said. "I want to see where she signed and while you're at it, get the other girl's too."

The man spun in a daze for a moment and then seemed to remember. He went naked to a briefcase in the opposite corner of the room that I hadn't noticed before. He came back waving a sheath of papers in his fat hand. "Signed, and all legal," the guy said. A trickle of sweat ran down his brow and across his shiny face. He ignored it.

I snatched the pages from out of the guy's hand, and tore them into shreds without even glancing at them.

"Hey!" the guy started to protest.

I snapped at him. "Shut up!" I spat the words like venom.

I looked past his shoulder to where the young woman lay on the mattress. She had her knees pressed together now, and had wrapped her hands over her body in a pathetic attempt to cover herself. She was staring back at me with dull out-of-focus eyes. I turned my attention back to the guy. I wrapped one muscled arm around the back of the man's neck in a kind of headlock and pulled him close so that only he could hear the menace in my voice.

"This is what's going to happen," I told him. "Both of these girls are going to walk out of here. Then you are going to erase the footage you have filmed of the girl on the bed." The guy started to get tense and I tightened the muscles in my forearms like a boa constrictor strangling a victim. "After you do that, I am going to film a promo for you. I will stand right beside you and tell the world what a good friend of mine you are and how great your films are."

The guy looked surprised.

"Then I'm going to hurt you."

The guy balked. His eyes became wide and fearful for a second as he realized what I'd said, and that I meant every word of it. He started to squirm, his sweating body slick and oily. I moved my arm so that there was pressure beneath his jaw, forcing his neck back until he was straining

251

against me, and his eyes grew very wide with panic.

"Okay," the guy went limp in a rush of breath. His arms flapped a little and then he stopped resisting. "Okay," he said again.

I helped the girl off the bed. She seemed dazed and unsteady on her feet. She fumbled her clothes on and teetered from the room without ever glancing back.

"Erase the tape," I ordered, "and put some fucking clothes on."

The guy snatched up the camera he had been filming with. His fingers were trembling. He stabbed some buttons and offered the camera up to me. "All done," he said. "Take a look for yourself."

I looked. There was nothing left recorded. I grunted. The guy went to a pile of dirty unwashed clothes at the foot of the bed. He dressed quickly. "You really going to shoot a promo for me?"

I nodded. He shook his head like he couldn't believe it and then lowered his voice to a dramatic whisper. "Are you really going to hurt me?"

"Count on it," I said. I didn't give the guy any time to think. He had a battered old tripod. I set the camera up, stabbed the 'record' button and dragged the guy over to stand beside me. I wrapped an arm around his shoulder and in an instant my expression transformed.

"Hi," I smiled warmly towards the camera. "This is Rick Cassidy and I'm down town in L.A. with my good buddy Jimmy D." I gave the fat bastard a warm slap on the shoulder. "We are on the set of Jimmy's brand new film called

'Fuckable MILFS'. Jimmy has scoured the west coast of America looking for the hottest ladies and filming them just for you," my voice was warm and urbane and full of good will. I glanced at the guy. There was an uncertain smile on his face.

"You will want to watch this film," I enthused. "There's not a woman under forty and they're all red hot and horny as hell. Take it from me," I pointed at the camera and my smile broadened. "This will be a film you have got to see."

I crossed to the camera and thumped the buttons to stop recording. The guy looked at me with a pained wrought expression on his face. "Hey, man. I don't film MILFS. I film young stuff."

I smiled grimly. "Not anymore," I said. "Not ever again."

I held the camera up for the guy so he could check the playback, and as he took it from me I punched him hard in the guts. The guy made an 'ooomf!' sound of pain as all the air was crushed from his lungs. The camera fell from his nerveless fingers and skittered across the ground. He bent over and clutched at his guts and as he did, I lifted my fist in an uppercut that caught him squarely under the jaw. It was one of my better punches – my legs were perfectly balanced and I drove up from my hips with all my weight and muscle behind the blow. The guy's head snapped back and I heard something crunch and break. He began to topple backwards like a felled tree and I saw a spurt of bright red blood spill from his gaping mouth.

I had to be quick. He was falling, and I knew if he hit the ground he would never get up. I took a single stride and then drove my foot between his legs like I was punting from my own-end zone on fourth and long. My foot socked meatily into the guy's crotch and the sound of it was like meat being butchered. The guy managed a single keening squeal before he hit the ground.

I was panting. I could feel the trembling rush of adrenalin sizzle and boil in my blood. I felt a wild and reckless elation – and an overwhelming sense of justice.

I took three long breaths, felt the sense of satisfaction seep into my bones, and then I crossed the room in careful measured steps where Connie and her daughter sat watching, their expressions pale and aghast.

I squatted on my haunches and held out my hand. "Hi, Roxy. My name is Rick Cassidy. I'm a porn actor – and I'm a friend of your mother's."

The girl held her hand out to me as if I was some ghostly apparition. Her grip was limp in the way that most young girls shake hands. I noticed she had the same long delicate fingers as her mother. I smiled into her eyes. "Your mom wanted me to talk to you about the porn industry. She tells me you have aspirations of being an actress. Is that right?"

Roxy nodded her head mutely, and then said softly, "I know you. I saw some of your films."

Beneath the pretty face, the high cheekbones, the flawless smooth skin and the deep soulful eyes, I could see intelligence and resolve in the girl's face. "What makes you want to film porn movies?"

Roxy found her voice at last, but it was wavering and tremulous like she was in the grips of some kind of mild shock. "That guy," she pointed at the man I had left bleeding on the floor. "He… he told me I had the face and the figure to be a star."

I glanced over my shoulder. The guy was writhing on the ground, his hands clutched between his legs, curled up into the fetal position. I turned back to Roxy.

"Can I tell you something?" I asked gently.

Roxy nodded. She was staring into my eyes intently.

"The porn industry doesn't need you, honey. The porn industry doesn't need another fresh-faced nineteen-year-old girl, because we've got so many of them," I said. "Every day, all around the world, young girls like you get lured or drawn into this industry, and you know what?"

"What?" she asked softly.

"They all get told the same thing," I smiled to take the edge off my words and make them seem less pointed. "Every girl gets told exactly what you got told – and it's not true. That doesn't mean you're not pretty, and it doesn't mean that you don't have a great figure. But it does mean that you'll never be a star, because there are too many other girls just as pretty as you and just as desperate."

Roxy's expression folded into a frown like maybe she was thinking about what I said and deep down knew that it was the truth. She glanced at her mother and then turned her eyes back to me. She swallowed nervously. "But I actually do like porn," she said.

"Good!" I enthused. "Then watch it until your eyes bleed. Watch every movie you can get your hands on – just don't put yourself into one. It's not the lifestyle you want, and it's not the kind of thing you want in your past because one day you're going to meet a guy who is bright and handsome and charming – not as handsome as me –," she smiled, "but when that day comes," I smiled back, "you won't want something like this haunting you because it never goes away."

Roxy went back to frowning. Back to thinking.

"If you really do have a fascination for porn films, then you can still be involved in the industry, Roxy," I said suddenly. "We need talented makeup artists. We need people with vision and flare and creativity behind the cameras that film the scenes – and we need production people who have a good eye for editing footage and putting a film together. Think about that," I urged. "Think about a career behind the scenes if you really want to work around the world of porn."

She sat there with a serious look on her face for long moments. "Is that all I should know?" she asked, back-tracking the conversation. "Is having yourself on film and having that footage of you in your past the worst of it?"

I shook my head. "No," I said with sudden sad realization. "Roxy, the worst part about making porn films is that it desensitizes you, honey. You reach the point, sooner than you realize, when you forget how to tell the difference between lust and love. You lose intimacy. You lose yourself. You lose your soul," I said softly. "Adult films are supposed to capture sexual moments, but in the process they hold your heart hostage so that one day you wake up and you realize you don't know what love is, or you've forgotten how it feels and because of that, it leaves you empty."

I glanced at Connie. She was crying. Her lips quivered and her eyes were dewy with tears. She sniffed and dabbed at her cheek.

She looked at me like she was seeing me for the first time. I felt her hand reach for mine and squeeze tightly. "Thank you," she mouthed the words silently.

We stood up and I watched as Connie hugged her daughter in an emotional moment that I knew I'd probably never experience. They were both crying, soft weeping sobs of reconnection.

Epilogue.

I loved the silence of this place. I stood on the balcony of the villa, staring up at the dark moonless sky. The night was filled with a million stars and all around me, the rolling French countryside was quiet.

I carried my drink inside and set it on the kitchen table. I went into the living area. Connie had slipped off her shoes and was dozing in front of the fireplace. I leaned over the back of the chair and kissed her upside-down face gently on the cheek.

She woke with a start and glanced around to find me.

"You're tired," I said.

"I was just resting my eyes."

"You were snoring."

There was a spark in her eyes. "I don't snore."

"I remember the night in L.A. after we had dinner at that little restaurant and I brought you home drunk and undressed you. You snored that night."

She folded her arms and there was a smile at the memory. "I only have your word for that," she challenged.

Roxy drifted into the living room with a makeup box in her hand. She set it inside the front door and then looked at us with a shrug. "I have a bad memory," she smiled. "I don't want to forget it in the morning. It's not going to make a good impression if I turn up on my first day of classes and I forgot to bring my makeup, right?"

I nodded. It had been six weeks since Connie and Roxy had followed me to Europe to live with me, and in that time we had settled into a routine that somehow seemed to work. "I will drop you off early," I promised. "I need to be down at the lake in the morning anyhow," I said. "Just make sure you're ready to leave on time, okay? I have a lot of actresses arriving on set tomorrow and I need to be back to start filming. If I'm late, they'll get into the booze and I won't get anything on film."

Roxy nodded. She smiled at her mom and then wandered away towards her bedroom. Connie watched her disappear down the hallway.

"I think I am tired," she said when we were alone. She yawned. There were several newspapers spread across her knees and a half-filled notepad on the armrest of the chair. She folded the papers carefully and then stood up.

"Deadline?" I asked.

She shrugged. "I still have two weeks before I need to submit," she said casually. She was working as a freelance journalist now, still writing articles for '*Infinity*' magazines but also writing for a couple of French publications and an online blog in Italy. She didn't seem to miss L.A. life at all.

"Sleep well," I said. She smiled, lifted herself on tiptoes and kissed me chastely on the lips. I watched her until she gently pushed her bedroom door closed behind her and then I went back to the kitchen and refilled my glass.

Outside the night air was cooling. I found the brightest star in the glittering sky and muttered a silent wish.

This wasn't love – I knew that. Connie, Roxy and I were living together and it was good, but what Connie and I had wasn't love.

But it was a start...

Also available by Jason Luke:
'Interview with a Master'

Printed in Great Britain
by Amazon.co.uk, Ltd.,
Marston Gate.